Living at Langster Motel

By

Cindy Sabulis

Copyright © 2021 by Cindy Sabulis

All rights reserved. Printed in the United States of America.

This is a work of fiction. Names, characters, places, and incidents are products of the author's imagination or if real, are used fictitiously.

No part of this publication may be reproduced, distributed, or transmitted in any form or by any means, including photocopying, recording, or other electronic or mechanical methods without the prior written permission of the author, except by reviewers who may quote brief passages in book reviews.

Published by Toat Publishing,
a division of Toys of Another Time, L.L.C.
Cover photo by Jina Rowland and M. C. Rowland

First Edition

Residents of Langster Motel

Cali Jarvis – *13 years old*
Phoenix Jarvis – *15 years old*
Georgia Jarvis – *9 years old*
Mrs. Jarvis – *Their mom*

~

Rivka Christianson – *13 years old*
Shannon Christianson – *15 years old*
Stacey Christianson – *9 years old*
Pauly Christianson – *5 years old*
Mr. and Mrs. Christianson - *Their parents*

~

Isabella Azar – *8 years old*
Reza Azar – *7 years old*
Mr. and Mrs. Azar - *Their parents*

~

Michael Fitzpatrick – *17 years old*
Mr. and Mrs. Fitzpatrick - *His parents*

~

Andrew and Brian Hudson – *3 years old*
Benjamin Hudson – *2 years old*
Julianna Hudson – *newborn baby*
Jodi Hudson – *Their 22-year-old mom*

~

Hakeem Jones – *10 years old*
Delilah Jones – *6 years old*
Trinika Jones – *3 years old*
Mrs. Jones– *Their mom*

~

Roberto Rivera – *10 years old*
Gabby Rivera – *8 years old*
Hector Rivera – *6 years old*
Mrs. Rivera– *Their mom*

~

Anita Sullivan – *9 years old*
Dwight Sullivan – *7 years old*
Mr. and Mrs. Sullivan - *Their parents*

~

Old Man Malcolm – *Older than dirt*

Classmates
Phoebe Watkins, Natalie Picolari, Hailey Ungerman, Cassandra Wolcott, Bernice Logan, Monica Reilly

Chapter 1

It was still dark outside when my fifteen-year-old sister shook me from a sound sleep. "Cali, get out of the bathroom," she said. "I need to take a shower."

"Leave me alone," I grumbled, pulling the sweatshirt I was using for a blanket over my head.

"Get up, Cali!" Phoenix yelled, pulling the sweatshirt off my face. "...and who said you could wear my cat nightshirt?"

Without answering, I picked up my pillow and crawled out of the tub. I felt like I'd been hit by a truck, which definitely wasn't a good way to start my first day of eighth grade in a new school.

"Why were you sleeping in the tub anyway?" Phoenix asked.

"Because it was impossible to sleep in our bed with you snoring like a congested walrus."

"That wasn't me snoring. That was Mom."

"Yeah, she was snoring too. And Georgia was whistling through her nose again like she was playing a flute or something."

"Well, just 'cause you couldn't sleep was no reason to wake the rest of us up," Phoenix said, pushing me out of the bathroom.

It wasn't like I purposely woke everyone up. After several hours of trying to fall asleep last night, I couldn't take the noise anymore, so I grabbed my pillow and headed for the bathroom. I tried to take the blanket off our bed too, but Phoenix had it wrapped around her so tightly I couldn't pull it off, so I had to settle for using a sweatshirt. Then my only choices for a bed were on the layers of dirty clothes that were all over the bathroom floor, or in the tub where I was less likely to be stepped on if someone came in to use the bathroom. I chose the tub, but turned out, it was still wet from my nine-year-old sister Georgia and her friend Stacey giving their dolls a bath earlier—only I didn't notice until I was lying down and felt something cold and wet inching up the back of my pajamas. I jumped up, but too late.

Naturally, I had to get dry pajamas out of the dresser, and the first thing I came up with was Phoenix's cat-print nightshirt. It was dark and I thought it was mine, but...oh, well. While I was fighting to close the dresser drawer, it let out a screeching protest and all the members of the Night-Time Nose & Mouth Orchestra were briefly jarred out of their snore fest long enough to yell at me for waking *them* up. I have to admit, waking them up was a well-deserved consolation prize since it was their fault I was awake in the first place.

After Phoenix commandeered the bathroom, I tried to sneak in another hour of sleep before I had to get ready for school, but as soon as I settled in my bed, Georgia woke up, then Mom got up, and believe me, there is *no* sleeping in the room once everyone else is awake.

At 7:25, there was a knock on our motel room door.

"You ready?" my friend Rivka asked when I opened the door.

"I'm not sure. Does this outfit look okay?" I had already changed three times, but nothing I owned looked right to me.

"It looks fine," Rivka said, barely glancing at what I was wearing. Considering she had on tattered jeans, a plain black tee-shirt, and sneakers splattered with paint the same barf green as the walls of her bedroom, I knew better than to ask her opinion. I tried to smooth some wrinkles in my skirt using my hands as an iron, did one last check for holes in my tights, then followed Rivka out the door.

"We need to come up with a reason why we're picked up in front of a motel," I said, as the two of us walked to the end of the parking lot to wait for the bus. "...in case anyone asks."

Rivka thought about it for a moment. "We can say we live over near Sultan Street, but we walk over here for the bus."

"Won't the kids that live near Sultan Street wonder why we walk all this way?"

A gust of wind blew Rivka's blond tumbleweed hair all over the place, but instead of having a massive panic attack trying to keep it neat like I was doing with my own hair, Rivka just let nature lash out at her curls.

"We could tell everyone one of our parents works down the road, and we ride in with them. We'll say this is the closest stop to their work," she suggested, tossing her head around a little to get the curls out of her face.

"It wouldn't make sense that we both go into work with them, would it?"

"Okay. How about we're training for a marathon, and every morning before school we run five miles from our house, and this is where we end up?"

"Yeahhhh...no," I said looking down at the skirt I was wearing. "I don't think that one is at all believable."

"Fine. You come up with something 'cause that's all I've got."

Last week, Rivka and I made a pact that even if someone held us down and forced us to eat day-old cafeteria fish-stick tacos, neither of us would ever tell anyone at school that we live in a motel. Unfortunately, having the bus stop right in front of it might be a giveaway.

"Okay. How about this? Our story will be that we live in a house beyond the woods that are in the back of the motel," I said. "Hopefully, if there really are houses there, no one on the bus already lives in them."

"That might work," Rivka said.

Three months ago, I really *was* living in a house, enjoying my own room and a luxury called *Privacy*. Now I'm stuck in a single room at this loser motel, sharing a double bed with my older sister Phoenix, just an arm's length away from my mother and my little sister Georgia, who sleep in the bed next to us.

After Mom and Dad had their last big showdown, Mom told us girls to hurry and pack only what we could fit in the car because we were leaving Dad and the only home we ever knew. In less than half an hour, my entire thirteen-year-old life was compressed into one suitcase, a backpack, and three plastic bags, then jammed into the trunk of our car next to my sisters' packed-up lives. Mom drove for hours, barely keeping us from the claws of starvation until she finally stopped at McDonald's for food and a much-needed bathroom break. Then it was back on the road until she stopped here at *Loser Motel*.

Okay, Loser Motel isn't really the name of this place—it's actually Langster Motel, but all the room doors have a big "L" on them. Every time I see them, all I think about that "L" standing for is *Loser*. This loser motel is *even* shaped like an "L." Talk about ironic.

Mom told us we needed to start our new lives where no one knew anything about our past. She said it would be too embarrassing to stay anywhere near Bronstonville since everyone there would know all about her breakup with Dad. So, here we are living like homeless squatters in a dumpy motel room in the dumpy town of Westernton, New York. Nothing to be embarrassed about there, right?

"Here comes the bus!" Rivka said, as soon as she spotted it turning the corner.

"Now don't forget, Rivka. Our houses are over there." I tossed my head in the direction of the woods behind the motel.

As we boarded the bus for Lincoln Middle School, I praised the gods of fortune because for the first time in forever, they were finally on my side.

"Can you believe it?" I said after we settled in our seats in the back of the bus.

We high-fived each other, relieved we didn't have to explain our motel bus stop to anyone.

"I knew all along we'd be the first stop," Rivka said.

"You did not! You were just as worried as I was."

"Well...I had a feeling we'd be first."

"Oh, you and your feelings..."

Rivka Christianson and I have only known each other since the beginning of summer, but it's like we've been best friends forever. The night my family arrived at the motel, Rivka was sitting outside the office watching us unpack our car. I assumed she was about my age, so naturally, I was curious and snuck peeks over at her. After the car was unloaded and my sisters were in the room calling dibs on which bed they got, I hung outside making sure nothing else was left in the car. Rivka came over and plopped herself down in the patio chair near our room. She had curly blond hair that ran wild on her head and freckles splattered over every visible part of her body.

"Six months," she said.

I waited for her to say something else, but when she didn't, I asked, "What's six months?"

"I predict you'll be here for six months."

"We're only here for the night," I informed her, smoothing my own hair to be sure it didn't look anything like the roll of tumbleweed that had landed on her head.

"Trust me," she said. "I have this sixth sense about guests who stay one night and those who end up staying for a year."

"Does this sixth sense have anything to do with how much stuff people remove from their cars and carry into their rooms?"

She folded her arms. "What? You don't believe me?"

I shrugged. "No, it's just we're definitely not going to be here six months."

She watched me as I looked beneath the seats of the car to see if anything had slipped under them.

"There's nothing under there," she informed me. Then she told me how she had this psychic ability in which she knew things before they happened and could see things other people couldn't. I had never met anyone with psychic ability before, and I wasn't quite sure I believed in it, but she was right--there wasn't anything under the seats.

"Well, since you're going to be here awhile, you might as well tell me your name," she said after I finished checking out the whole car.

"California," I told her. It appeared her psychic ability didn't include guessing people's names or she would have already known the answer.

"I didn't ask where you were from. I asked your name."

"California IS my name. But everyone calls me Cali."

"Were you born in California?" she asked.

"No. Never been there." *Obviously*, she wasn't a very good psychic.

"Why were you named after a state you've never been to?" she asked.

"My parents are weird," I explained. "They've never been to Phoenix, Arizona or the state of Georgia either, but they named my sisters after those places."

She nodded like she got it, then said, "My name's Rivka."

I tried to look as if I thought Rivka was a perfectly normal name, but I think she read my mind and knew it was a name I wouldn't want.

"It's a *nice* Jewish name," she explained.

"You're Jewish?"

Rivka shook her head. "Not at all."

"Then why do you have a Jewish name?" I asked.

"Because I have weird parents too."

From that moment on, Rivka and I were like two pieces of Velcro stuck together. How could I not be best friends with someone who has a weirder name than mine? Let's face it—California Jarvis isn't your Jane Normal kind-of-name, but at least it's not as bad as Rivka Christianson. I mean, who gives their kid a Jewish first name to go with the last name Christianson? At least my last name wasn't Massachusetts or Montana, or something like that. California Montana...I can't even imagine.

In addition to our unique (as in weird) names, there are plenty of other things Rivka and I have in common. For example, we both have an older sister who is obsessed with boys, especially ones who have their licenses. And we both have nine-year-old sisters who bug the beans out of us. However, the one thing Rivka has my undying sympathy for is that she also has a little brother. Rivka's brother Pauly is more irritating than all four of our sisters put together. Ever since I first laid eyes on that buzzed-cut kid I can honestly say I am thankful I don't have a younger brother.

Rivka's been living at the motel for almost two years. Her father is the manager here, hired by the company who owns the motel. Rivka told me that "Motel Manager" is just a fancy title for caretaker, because that's really what Mr. Christianson is. He takes care of everything at the motel, from manning the front desk, to mowing the grass in the side yard, to changing burnt out light bulbs around the parking lot. Although her mother doesn't actually get paid for the work she does around the motel, she's sort of a caretaker too. She handles the front desk when Mr. Christianson isn't around, works in the laundry room, and cleans the rooms on the rare occasions when people actually check out of the motel. Prior to being the Motel Manager, Rivka's father was unemployed for more than a year before he got this job—which came with the added benefit of a rent-free, four-and-a-half-room apartment behind the office where the Christianson family lives.

The apartment has a living room, a kitchen, two bedrooms, and a bathroom with a lock on the door. Talk about lucky! Of course, Rivka doesn't think she's lucky, but I'll give her one night of sleeping in my casket size, snore-infested motel room with no lock on the bathroom door, and you mark my word, she'll go back to her apartment feeling like she just won the New York Home Lottery.

Rivka and I sat in the back of the bus watching the kids get on at every stop. As the bus filled up, the level of noise grew as the kids getting on hooked up with their old friends. It was obvious most of the kids knew each other. Other than an occasional glance in our direction, everyone ignored us. I was hoping we didn't look like the awkward newbies we really were.

"There's our new school," I said to Rivka when the bus finally pulled into the parking lot of Lincoln Middle School.

Rivka stared out the window at the red brick building. "I'm starting to wish I was still being homeschooled," she said nervously.

"You'll do fine," I assured her. "We'll both do fine."

Up until now, Rivka and her sisters had been homeschooled, but this year her little brother was starting kindergarten and the idea of trying to teach him was more than their mother could handle, so she registered all the Christianson kids for public school for the first time. Rivka had some anxiety about going to regular school, and last week, when the two of us were having a sleepover together in one of the empty motel rooms, she nearly had a full-blown panic attack about it. I tried to calm her fears by telling her all the good things about school, leaving out all the bad stuff so as not to scare her any more than she already was. Bad stuff like having kids not like you just because you made good grades, or having everyone in your class think you're the teacher's pet even if you tried to prove you weren't by writing "I HATE MRS. MANITO" on the board on a dare from Jessica Mattern when Mrs. Manito left the room.

Those were things that happened at my old school, but I left them out as I assured Rivka our new school was going to be great and we were going to make lots of new friends. I spent an hour that night trying to convince her that school was tons better than it really was, and I thought Rivka was okay with the idea of going after that. Until now, that is.

"I still have a bad feeling about this place, Cali."

"That's just first-day-of-school jitters. I have them too. Everyone gets them."

"I hope they go away soon, because I'm not liking the feeling."

Rivka and I got off bus and we instantly got caught up in the riptide of students heading into the building. Once inside, I pulled Rivka out of the stream of kids, and the two of us stood against the wall for a few moments surveying our surroundings.

"One good thing about starting school here is that we have no history following us," I said, trying to calm my own first-day jitters. "And who knows? Without any history weighing us down, maybe we could become the most popular girls at this school."

Rivka chuckled and seemed to relax a little. "You dream big, Cali."

"No, really. It's possible," I said, lowering my voice, "...as long as no one here finds out we live in a motel."

Chapter 2

After school, Rivka and I were hiding out on the back steps of the motel, rehashing the first day of school.

"I still can't believe we ended up in the same class," Rivka said.

"I know! Maybe that's a sign that good things are going to happen this year."

As we were talking, Mrs. Jones, who lives in Room 16, peeked around the corner of the motel. She is a large-sized woman who always wears colorful clothing, and even though we hoped she couldn't see us, there was no missing her. When she spotted me and Rivka attempting to stay out of her line of vision, she walked over to us, with her two little girls trailing behind.

Now, it's bad enough living in a motel swarming with younger kids, but apparently being thirteen-years old is prime age for babysitting and whether or not we like it, Rivka and I are considered the Disney Destination of Babysitters for parents around the motel. No one ever asks my sister Phoenix or Rivka's fifteen-year-old sister Shannon to babysit because everyone knows high school girls are way too busy doing homework (not!) or way too busy thinking about boys that they can't be relied on. Apparently, eighth graders are the perfect victims to be taken advantage of by parents desperate to get away from their offspring, and since Rivka and I are the only two kids at the motel old enough to babysit but not old enough to be seriously dating, we always get stuck babysitting all the little brats who live here.

The total combined babysitting income the two of us made the whole summer comes to $0 because the number of parents who live in this motel who actually pay middle school sitters to watch their kids is also a big fat zero. All the parents here expect us to watch their kids for free. They figure because we are already hanging around outside the motel and the little critters they hatched are outside, it's no big deal for us to watch them. Ha!

Mrs. Jones came right up to the steps where we were sitting, obviously not fooled by our secret hiding place. She is a single mom living in the motel with her ten-year old son Hakeem and two daughters, Delilah who's six and Trinika who's three. She has a southern accent and calls everyone Honey or Sugar or some other good-tasting food. She even calls her own kids things like Pumpkin or Cupcake. Whenever Mrs. Jones is around, it doesn't take long for my mouth to start watering and my stomach to start growling for something to eat.

"Would y'all keep an eye on my L'il Apple Dumplin's for me?" Mrs. Jones said with her southern drawl. She was wearing a billowing flowered dress that would scare off a clown and an oversized feathery hat that looked like a large purple bird died on top of it. "I'm fixing to run a few errands, and it's so much quicker without the sweet l'il ones along."

If my mouth hadn't started watering for apple dumplings at that exact moment, I probably would have opened it to tell her we were way too busy to watch her kids. If she were my own mother, I would have flat-out refused, but she was someone else's mother and I didn't have the nerve.

"Come, on," I said to the scrawny little girls who looked nothing like apple dumplings, "let's go play in the sand box."

"So much for this hiding place..." Rivka muttered.

"Y'all *shore* are peaches," Mrs. Jones said. "I shouldn't be more than an hour."

Ha! Our mushy peach brains had heard that one a tree load of times before.

"Hakeem is around here some place," Mrs. Jones said. "Just let him know where I went."

"We have to watch Hakeem too?" Rivka groaned.

"Do *yew* mind?" Mrs. Jones asked in her syrupy voice.

I took Trinika by the hand, figuring she was smaller and easier to handle than her older sister, but Trinika's hand was sticky from pieces of lollipop still attached to her, and I instantly regretted picking her over Delilah. Rivka, not realizing how lucky she was to get the lesser-sticky kid, took Delilah's relatively clean hand. As we started towards the front of the motel with the two little girls, we were nearly plowed down by ten-year-old Roberto Rivera as he rocketed around the corner.

"ROBERTO!" his mother's voice screeched from the front of the motel. "GET BACK HERE THIS MINUTE!"

"I DIDN'T DO IT, MA!" he yelled.

The height-challenged Mrs. Rivera appeared around the corner of the building, hurrying as fast as her high-heeled shoes would allow.

"Get over here, now!" she yelled at her son. She pointed to a spot in front of her.

Without a flea-size chance for escape, Roberto dragged himself over to his mother. Mrs. Rivera's high heels gave her the added height she needed to yell closer to the face of her five-foot-tall son. "I don't ever want to catch you scaring your sister like that again, do you hear me?"

Roberto wiped his mother's spit spray off his face. "Yeah—I hear ya! I hear ya!"

Seizing him by the arm, Mrs. Rivera pulled her son over to us. Her frosted auburn hair had a greenish tint to it, making it look like tarnished copper. "Girls, I need you to keep an eye on Roberto," she said.

Rivka held up Delilah's little hand she was holding and fake-regretfully said, "Sorry, we're already watching the Jones kids." We both looked over to Mrs. Jones for confirmation and an out.

"I know that," Mrs. Rivera said. "Mrs. Jones and I are going to the store together. Gabby and Hector are both playing in the side yard so you'll have to go watch them there." She pushed Roberto in front of us. "And make sure *this* one stays out of trouble."

Mrs. Jones put her arm around Mrs. Rivera's shoulders. "*Hunny*, why't we stop and have us a nice cup of coffee 'fore we head to the grocery store."

Translation: Free babysitters, free time on their hands, back sometime before Rivka and I graduate from high school.

The two of them walked away trying to decide whether to bask in their freedom at Starbucks or The Coffee House.

As soon as they were out of sight, Roberto cried, "See ya!" and took off running.

"Roberto! Get back here!" Rivka yelled to his fleeing back.

Now, normally, a kid who is ten years old doesn't need a thirteen-year-old babysitter to watch him while he plays outside, but Roberto Rivera isn't a normal kid. He's the kind of kid any mother would be glad she didn't have. According to my own mother, Mrs. Rivera doesn't like to leave Roberto alone too long out of fear he'll burn down the motel or something. Any time he's not watched, he manages to damage or destroy something, and when his mother finds out, he always denies he had anything to do with it. Of course, Mrs. Rivera knows better. She even yells at him for things he didn't do because she assumes he did it anyway. Rivka and I hate keeping an eye on him because even though Mrs. Rivera knows her son is as destructive as a high-speed bulldozer, she'll be yelling her mouth off at us too if Roberto gets into trouble while we're supposed to be watching him.

"Okay...how we going to watch him if we can't even see him?" I asked, struggling with Trinika who was tugging my arm out of its socket and whining about wanting to play in the sandbox.

Rivka shrugged. "I'm not gonna worry about him. For all I care, he can stay away until he's old enough to shave."

"Play...ground! Play...ground!" Delilah chanted, pulling Rivka's hand to hurry her along. Trinika copied her older sister and started pulling me. "Play...ground! Play...ground!" she cried.

"Pipe down, little monkeys," Rivka pleaded, even though she allowed Delilah to lead her over to the side yard.

The side yard is the closest thing to a playground we have at the motel, which isn't saying much. It's a pitiful patch of lawn next to the front parking lot with a disintegrating sandbox, a rusting swing set, and a couple of maple trees thirteen-year-old babysitters can sit under to at least stay shaded while they wither away in boredom.

The Jones sisters ran over to the sandbox, and before Rivka and I even had a chance to collapse under a tree, two other little girls from the motel started screaming on the other side of the yard. Roberto's younger brother Hector was chasing his sister Gabby and Isabella Azar from Room 8 with a small garden snake. The normally quiet girls were screaming in terror.

"HECTOR!" Rivka hollered across the yard. "Leave those girls alone!"

Six-year-old Hector threw the snake into a bush and shouted, "I didn't do anything!"

"I don't know why Hector has to copy everything his big brother does," I said.

"For some stupid reason, he idolizes Roberto," Rivka said.

"Well, between the two of them, they're going to cause their mother's green hair to turn gray."

While Hector ran away from the scene of the crime, the two snake-terrified girls were clutching each other, and acting like they had just come face-to-face with death.

"You going to take care of the two crybabies over there?" Rivka asked.

Rivka doesn't handle crying kids very well so that task is usually left to me. I walked over to Gabby and Isabella, whose sobs were way overdone considering the garden snake wasn't much bigger than an earthworm.

"Calm down, girls, the snake is gone and so is Hector."

Sandwiched between the two Rivera boys is their eight-year-old sister Gabby, a pretty little girl with huge dark eyes and long black hair. Rivka and I are convinced that when Gabby was born, she was delivered to the wrong family because she is nothing like the other three loud-mouthed Riveras. You'd think with a name like Gabby she'd talk nonstop, but it appears to have had the opposite effect on her. I'm guessing she is so quiet because her green-haired mother is yelling all the time, and her demonic brothers are always shouting they didn't do something, there's little hope of anyone hearing her even if she did say something. Even though Gabby doesn't talk a lot, she screams and cries quite a bit thanks to her two brothers who enjoy terrorizing her and her friends.

"I...want...my...mommy," Gabby choked out in a tiny voice.

I glanced at the back of Mrs. Jones' car as it disappeared out of the parking lot, off on a freedom adventure.

"Your mother will be back soon," I tried to convince her. Based on her mother's past outings, I knew "soon" would be hours. The two single moms would probably park themselves in a coffee shop somewhere and yak away for hours about the husbands they no longer had. Mrs. Rivera was grieving the loss of a husband who went to an early grave and Mrs. Jones was dealing with a husband who probably left her for a skinnier woman who didn't wear clown-scaring outfits.

"Why don't you girls go play on the swings?" I said, hoping the distraction would make them forget about snakes and absent mothers.

The two girls held hands and headed over to the swings, their tear-filled eyes darting around the yard, fearful of another attack from Hector or some other snake-wielding boy.

I headed back to where Rivka was sitting on the ground getting ready for a long afternoon of watching a bunch of kids who lived in the motel.

"There has to be something better for us than this," I said to Rivka, waving my arm around the yard.

"Face it, Cali. We're doomed," Rivka said.

"No, we're not! We're not going to spend eighth grade just sitting around this motel watching these kids all day."

"So, what do you suggest?" Rivka asked.

"Well, once we start making friends at school, we can do things with them. Go places with them. Get away from this motel."

"Sounds good to me," Rivka said.

"...And, since we're making new friends anyway, we're going to start by making friends with the popular kids. I've spent my whole life being one of the underdogs at school. It's time to cozy up to the other side."

"I'm game," Rivka said. "Let's be popular."

"Yeah. Let's be popular!" I repeated.

I knew just saying it or even just hoping for it wasn't going to make it happen, but I had enough of feeling like a nobody at my old school. I was going to do whatever it took not to feel that way in my new school.

Chapter 3

The next day during lunch, Rivka and I sat in the cafeteria observing our targets.

"Those are the girls we need to get in good with," I whispered to Rivka, tossing my head in the direction of the table where four girls from our class sat: Phoebe Watkins, Natalie Picolari, Hailey Ungerman, and Cassandra Wolcott.

"Those are the girls who snickered when the teachers called out your name," Rivka pointed out.

It wasn't the first time I'd been laughed at for having an unusual name, but now I was older and I wasn't going to let it get to me.

"Somehow we have to make them like us," I said, trying my hardest to ignore the fact that the girls thought the name California Jarvis was funny.

Natalie Picolari, Hailey Ungerman, and Cassandra Wolcott were like royalty—pretty and stylish, and everyone seemed in awe of them. I began thinking of them as the Royal Rulers of Lincoln Middle School. But the girl I really wanted to make friends with was Phoebe Watkins. She was the *Royal'est* of the Rulers.

"I don't think I've ever seen anyone with magenta hair before," Rivka said, staring across the room at Queen Phoebe, whose short nylon jacket almost matched her hair color.

"That's called style," I said.

"I call it mistake with a bottle of hair dye." Rivka squinted her eyes for a better look.

"It wasn't a mistake," I said. "She's going for that unique look. And don't make it so obvious that you're staring at her."

While Rivka and I pretended to look everywhere but at the Royal Ruler's table, we took note of everything they wore, and everything they did. Phoebe had her hands underneath the table, and was staring down at them, and I suspected she was texting on a cell phone under the table—a definite no-no at school.

"What do you think about the way Natalie's dressed?" Rivka asked.

Natalie reminded me a little of Ariana Grande, but not quite as pretty. She was wearing a pair of pink skinny jeans, a long lacey white shirt with a gold belt, and large hoop earrings.

"I think Natalie's also very stylish, but not in the same way that Phoebe is," I observed.

"It kind of bothers me that she's rich and flaunting it," Rivka said, staring at the cafeteria wall several tables away from the Royals in her attempt not to look too obvious.

"What makes you think she's rich?"

Rivka turned to me and rolled her eyes. "Oh, pa-leeze! Her outfit just screams dollar signs."

"What do you know about expensive clothes?" I asked, tugging on Rivka's oversized tee-shirt.

"Even I can tell she doesn't buy her clothing from the Dollar Store."

"I'm guessing Cassandra's outfit is way more expensive than Natalie's," I said. "I love her turquoise Ugg boots."

Rivka risked another look over at the Royal's table, craning her head to try to see Cassandra's feet.

"Why is she wearing boots anyway?" Rivka asked, looking away again. "It's only September."

"Dramatic impact, I guess." Even if I hadn't overheard Cassandra in homeroom this morning bragging to Natalie about how she played the part of Little Red over the summer in a community production of "Into the Woods" I would have figured out Cassandra was all about the drama. Every wave of her hand, every tilt of her head said, "I am an actress."

"I have to tell you, Hailey the Hamster bugs me," Rivka said.

"Really, Rivka? A hamster?"

"She has eyes like a hamster and cheeks like a chipmunk."

"Ouch, you're being harsh."

"I'm just being honest. Plus, I'm having a hard time getting past all her neediness."

"What neediness?"

"Her need for approval from everyone," Rivka explained. "Haven't you noticed how she pouts like a baby if people don't agree with her?"

"Yeah, I guess that is a little annoying," I admitted.

"And that chipmunk voice of hers is annoying too," Rivka added.

Monica Reilly from our class came up to our table, and Rivka and I had to abandon our Royal Family watching.

"Anyone sitting here?" Monica asked, looking at the empty seats around us.

We both shook our heads.

In just one day, I already had Monica pegged as the class nerd. She kind of reminded me of myself, or rather what I used to be, last year. Sitting at the same table with her during lunch definitely wasn't going to improve our chances at getting in with the Royal Rulers.

Before she sat down, Monica frantically waved to Bernice Logan who was zig-zagging around the cafeteria looking for an empty table. Bernice made her way over to us.

"Yay! For a minute there, I thought we were going to have to eat standing up," she said to Monica. Just as she sat down, she let out a torrent of rapid-fire sneezes.

I held my breath and tried not to breathe in any sneeze germs. Monica pulled a tissue from her purse and passed it to Bernice. "It's all those cats you have," she said. "You're allergic to them."

"I'm not allergic to cats," Bernice said, wiping her watery eyes. "I've had them my whole life, and they've never bothered me."

"You've been sneezing obsessively your whole life," Monica pointed out.

"I don't sneeze obsessively," said Bernice. As if just saying the word made her do so, she sneezed several more times. "It's just there's a lot of pollen in the air right now," she sniffed.

Monica looked over at Rivka who was fearlessly gobbling down her hot lunch.

"Where did you guys go to school last year?" she asked.

"I was homeschooled," Rivka said, her mouth full of chicken fillet sandwich. She picked a piece of lettuce off her chin and popped it in her mouth before adding, "My mom homeschooled me and my sisters from the time we were old enough to hold a book in our hands."

I tried to send Rivka a telepathic message to warn her that her eating habits were gross and wouldn't help our chances of getting in with anyone, no less the popular group. I even kicked her under the table for additional emphasis, but she just stared at me completely baffled. So much for her psychic ability.

"I guess that's why we don't remember seeing you before," Monica said. "Why aren't you being homeschooled this year?"

"My parents figured it was time we mainstream into public school," Rivka said. "So, here I am." She eliminated the part about her mother figuring none of the Christianson girls would learn a lick of anything if all her time was spent trying to harness Pauly down and forcing him to learn something from a book.

"What about you?" Monica asked me. "Were you homeschooled last year too?"

"No, I just moved here the beginning of summer," I said, brushing my fingers across my chin to be sure nothing was hanging from it. "I used to live in Bronstonville, New Jersey."

"Never heard of it," Bernice said.

"I never heard of Westernton, New York until I moved here," I replied.

"How do you like living here?" Monica asked.

I couldn't tell her the truth; that living in a single motel room sucked sour pickles.

"Well...," I said picking my words carefully, "so far school's not too bad, but I really miss having my own room." As far as understatements go, that comment registered way below sea level.

Monica nodded. "Yeah, I know how that is. I have to share a room with my sister. It totally stinks."

"That's nothing," Rivka said. "I have to share a room with *two* sisters."

It was all I could do to keep from rolling my eyes at both of them. At least they didn't have to share their room with two sisters AND *their mother* like some people at the table did!

We ate our lunch, pretending to ignore the shrieks and giggles coming from the Royal Rulers' table. I kept sneaking peeks over there, wondering what they were laughing at, and hoping it wasn't the name California Jarvis.

Monica briefly glanced over at their table and sighed. "Looks like another year of listening to that," she said.

Rivka and I sat there waiting for her to explain, and when she didn't the psychic Rivka asked, "What do you mean?"

Monica threw her head towards the Royal Rulers. "Those girls think they're the school's greatest gift and they want everyone to know it."

"They do seem rather confident," I said, trying to be polite.

"That's not confidence. That's conceit."

Rivka gave me a told-you-so look.

"Natalie Picolari practically invented conceit," Monica added. "She thinks because she's so rich, it entitles her to treat everyone else like they are beneath her."

"She's rich?" Rivka asked innocently. "Who would have thought?" She gave me another one of her told-you-so looks.

Ignoring Rivka, I asked. "What about Phoebe? She doesn't seem too bad."

"Whatever you do, stay away from her too," Monica warned, lowering her voice.

"Why?" I asked.

Monica's eyes pierced into mine, and she said dead serious, "Phoebe bites if you get too close."

The bell rang, signaling the end of lunch period, and the end of finding out more information about Phoebe's biting habits.

"So...you think Phoebe really bites?" Rivka asked as we headed out of the cafeteria.

"I think Monica exaggerates just a little."

"Well...Phoebe does look kind of mean," Rivka answered.

In a fake British accent, I replied, "Queens must look mean. It helps keep their subjects in line."

Trying her hardest to sound British back, Rivka said, "The ladies-in-waiting look like they want to dethrone their ruler and take over the empire."

"Taking over the queendom means power. Money. Castles. Servants. Rivka, you and I are going to infiltrate that royal circle. And maybe someday, we will be queen and princess of this school."

"Which one of us will be queen, and which one princess?" Rivka asked.

"Maybe we'll be co-queens," I replied. "We'll figure it out later."

"Well, I better work some more on my royalty voice," Rivka said switching back to being British.

We walked to social studies yakking away in our newly-acquired British accents. We were so busy pretending we were British, we didn't even notice we had caught up to the Royal Rulers and were walking directly behind them. Of course, we noticed as soon as they stopped walking and I smacked right into Natalie's back.

She spun around, no longer looking like Ariana Grande, but more like Disney's Cruella de Vil. "Hey! Watch where you're going, klutz!"

I swear, it felt like everything came to a dead stop in the hallway and every kid was staring at me. Queen Phoebe glanced at me for only a moment before she continued off towards our social studies room, but Haley and Cassandra parked themselves next to Natalie with amused looks on their faces.

I felt the fire in my cheeks and hoped they didn't look as hot as they felt. "I...I'm...sorry," I stammered. "I didn't expect you to stop so suddenly."

"Next time, try keeping twelve paces back," Natalie said.

"Sorry," I said again.

I darted around the three Royals, and hurried down the hall with Rivka rushing to catch up.

"Well, I don't suppose that will help us get into their little clique," Rivka whispered in her fake British accent.

I felt like telling her to shut up, but my mouth seemed to be keeping twelve paces back.

Chapter 4

That weekend, Rivka and I were sitting on the back steps, once again hiding from babysitting-hungry parents. Ignoring everything Monica had told us, I was still determined to make friends with the popular girls.

"So now that the Royal Rulers know we're alive, we need to take some drastic action in order to enter their dynasty world," I said.

"More drastic than ramming into them in the hall?" Rivka asked.

"For the record, crashing into Natalie was a good way to get their attention," I said, trying to put a positive spin on the embarrassment of it all. "Now we need to impress them with a little less body contact."

"I got it!" Rivka cried. "Let's show them how awesome I am at predicting things. That should impress them."

"None of your predictions have ever come true."

"How about the time I predicted that the Langstermobile had a flat tire when my dad was late for that residents' meeting?"

"That morning your dad had mentioned the Langstermobile had a tire that looked low. Anyone could have guessed it would be flat by afternoon."

"Anyone but my dad," Rivka admitted.

The Langstermobile is a blood-red van that has a sign on top with the motel's name—kind of like one of those pizza delivery cars, only twice as big, and four times uglier. On the sides of the van are pictures of happy, well-dressed people who look nothing like anyone who actually lives at the motel. The fake van people are standing in front of a "Langster Motel" sign and look as if staying at the motel is the best thing that ever happened to them. The van is supposed to be for shuttling guests to and from the airport, but since guests who could actually afford to take a plane trip somewhere, could probably afford to stay in a better motel than this one, Mr. Christianson mostly uses the van to haul stuff from The Home Depot. Luckily, Rivka's parents also own a normal-looking beige Honda van that Mrs. Christianson can drive the kids in because if they didn't have that inconspicuous vehicle, the Christianson kids would rather die an exhausted pedestrian than be seen riding in the Langstermobile.

While Rivka and I tried to come up with a list of our redeeming qualities, our younger sisters Georgia and Stacey came out the back door of the Christiansons' apartment. Stacey was carrying a purple plastic case, and after the two girls sat down on the step above us Stacey opened it. It was filled with brushes, combs, barrettes, and elastic bands. She pulled out a hairbrush and started brushing Georgia's hair.

"Don't you have someplace else to go," Rivka snapped at her sister.

"Nope," Stacey replied. "Shannon won't let us play hairstylist in our room because she and Phoenix are hanging out in there."

Like Rivka, Stacey has blond hair, only hers is long and straight. She usually wears it in cockeyed pigtails or some other style she does herself, rather than go with the crazy tumbleweed look Rivka prefers.

"You can't hang out here," Rivka said.

"Why not? You don't own the steps." Her sister stopped brushing Georgia's hair to hunt around in her plastic case for an elastic band.

"Let them stay, Rivka," I said. "Maybe they can help us come up with something."

I took the pad of paper and pen we had brought out with us and numbered the paper 1 through 10.

"Mark my word, nothing good will come out of them helping," Rivka said.

Ignoring her, I turned to my sister. "If you had to say something good about us, what would it be?"

Georgia's brown eyes squinted in deep thought. "Hmmmm...you mean like you don't pick on me when I'm asleep?" she asked.

"I'm serious, Georgie. What do you like about me?"

"I like it that you don't pick on me when I'm asleep and you don't snore in my ear at night the way Mom does," said Georgia.

She and Stacey catapulted into a fit of laughter.

Rivka rolled her eyes. "See, I told you nothing good would come out of this. My prediction came true."

When they finally quit their squealing, Georgia said. "Okay...I've got something for real. I liked the time you two organized a scavenger hunt."

"Yeah, that was fun," Stacey agreed.

"See, Rivka! We have good organizational skills. That ought to count for something."

I wrote "Good organizational skills" after #1 on the list.

A few weeks ago, Rivka and I were feeling generous towards some of the kids at the motel, so we decided to organize a scavenger hunt for them. We had everyone get into teams and gave each team a list of things they had to find. The first team to find everything on the list won a pack of gum. Okay, the prize was a little lame, but still...it was pretty funny to watch all these little kids scurrying around the grounds of the motel like crazed monkeys, running from room to room asking everyone if they had anything on the list.

While the kids frantically looked for stuff around the motel, Rivka and I had a whole hour to ourselves to sit on the side lawn next to the parking lot and relax without being bothered by anyone. Once in a while a kid would come over and whine about how hard it was to find an aardvark in New York, then they'd stomp off mad when we'd tell them to quit their complaining and just keep looking. Rivka had put the aardvark on the list to make it more challenging, especially since half the kids didn't even know what an aardvark was, and she predicted no one would find one. But when the team consisting of Georgia, Stacey, Gabby Rivera, and Isabella Azar improvised and came up with a picture of an aardvark in a book they found in the Azars' room, I had a hard time convincing Rivka her prediction was wrong. She stood by her prediction and insisted it was 100% correct because no one came up with a *real* aardvark, but she did agree to declare the girls the winners of the pack of gum. The boys' team with Pauly Christianson, Reza Azar, Hakeem Jones, and Roberto and Hector Rivera were all sore losers. There was a lot of yelling and even some crying over the aardvark picture and the pack of gum. That's when Rivka and I went around to the back steps to get away from them all.

"How about we add that we're kind to little kids?" I asked.

"Not true!" Stacey said, pointing a comb at her sister. "Rivka's mean to me all the time."

"Yeah, and you're mean to me," Georgia added.

"Siblings don't count," I said. "We're kind to kids we're not related to."

"But you both hate kids you're not related to," Georgia said.

"I told you *nothing good* was going to come of them being here," Rivka pointed out.

"Okay...I suppose you're good at predicting some things," I finally admitted.

I scribbled down "Kind to kids" and "Good at predicting things" after #2 and #3 on our list.

"Okay. Let's go about this a different way. What good qualities would you like in a friend?" I asked the younger girls.

"They have to be nice," Georgia said, looking in a small hand mirror to examine the lopsided ponytail on her head.

"They have to be kind," Stacey added.

"And generous," said Georgia.

"And pretty," said Stacey, brushing one of her long pigtails.

"Pretty?" Georgia looked at her in surprise. "You like people just because they're pretty?"

"Well, I don't want to be friends with someone who looks like a monster," Stacey replied, looking at her profile in the small mirror.

"That's so mean!" Georgia cried. "You shouldn't like people just because of how they look. If someone looks like a monster, you shouldn't hate them for it."

"So, how many friends do you have who look like a monster?" Stacey asked.

"Well, none, but that's because I don't know any monster-looking kids."

"What about Roberto? Would you be friends with him?"

"Acting like a monster and looking like one are two different things."

I held up my hand to stop them. "Will you two quit and get back to traits you want in a friend."

"What's this list for anyway?" Georgia asked.

"We want to make friends with some kids at school, so we're trying to figure out what good traits we have that would make them want to be friends with us."

"Ha! Good luck with that," Stacey said, boxing up her hairstyling supplies.

"Yeah, you can't *make* someone like you," Georgia said. "They should just like you the way you are."

"Oh, you don't know anything," I said. "You're only nine."

I knew my sister had a point, but I wasn't going to admit it to her.

After the two of them left, I said to Rivka, "Let's hope the Royal Rulers like us for our good qualities, whatever they are."

"Well, if they don't, we can still organize a scavenger hunt for their siblings if we ever get stuck babysitting them," Rivka said.

I think she was kidding, but with Rivka, you can't always tell for sure.

Chapter 5

The next afternoon, Rivka and I were again hiding out on the back steps of the Christianson's apartment when we were sentenced to the dreaded babysitting task again, this time by my own mother.

"Cali, I'm taking Jodi to the clinic for a doctor's appointment," Mom yelled to me from the corner of the motel. "I told her you'd watch her boys while we're gone."

"Why does she volunteer me like that?" I moaned to Rivka.

Rivka smirked. "Obviously, she knows how much you love kids."

I hollered back, "We're really busy, Mom. Can't Phoenix watch them for a change?"

"Phoenix went to the thrift store with Shannon and Mrs. Christianson."

Rivka balled her hands into fists. "Wow! You'd think my own mother would have offered to take us shopping too—but, nope, this is the first I hear about it. Nice mother I have!"

"Yeah, well at least your mother isn't volunteering you to babysit like mine is."

"LET'S GO, CALI!" Mom yelled, her arms crossed in her don't-mess-with-my-patience way, "NOW!"

Jodi Hudson and her boys live in Room 15, the room next to ours.

"Seven months," Rivka predicted when she first arrived. That seven months wasn't how far along Jodi was in her pregnancy. That's how long Rivka expected Jodi and her kids to stay at the motel. Jodi has three boys; three-year-old twins Andrew and Brian and two-year old Benjamin. And she's pregnant with her fourth kid! Rivka found out from eavesdropping on her parents that Jodi's husband is in jail for hijacking a truck full of baby formula. Baby formula! Of all things. Now Jodi's serving her own sentence living alone in this motel with three and a half kids. It's just my dumb luck my mother likes to help her out by offering my servitude of free babysitting anytime Jodi needs it—which is pretty much every day.

"Even though you still owe me for helping you babysit the other day, I'll help you again," Rivka generously offered. "But I want half of whatever you get paid."

"But half of nothing is nothing," I pointed out, before I realized she was totally being sarcastic. "And besides, I was the one helping *YOU* babysit the other day."

"I'll keep an eye on Andrew and Brian while you go get Benny," Rivka said as we came around to the front of the motel. She headed over to the sandbox where the Hudson twins were playing, and I went over to the open door of Room 15. Jodi and her boys don't care much about privacy, and they often leave the door to their room wide open, even when the kids are getting dressed or taking a nap. Sometimes during the day, I'll walk by their room and see Jodi lying on the bed like she wants to take a nap herself, but her boys will be jumping on the bed or crawling all over her like a litter of puppies.

Even though the door was open, I knocked on the door frame before I went inside. Jodi sat on the end of one bed trying to reach around her ballooning stomach to tie her sneakers. Two-year old Benjamin was lying on the other bed, sucking his thumb and sleepily watching his mother.

"Is Benny going down for a nap?" I asked hopefully.

Jodi looked up at me with her basset hound eyes. Even though she is only 22 years old, she looks a whole lot older. Like about 32.

"No...he's just waking up," she said wearily. "Would you mind, Cali?" she asked, thrusting her untied shoe towards me. "I can't reach them."

As I tied her shoes, Jodi mentioned that Benjamin had slept for two hours. "He should be raring to go once he wakes up completely."

I bit my bottom lip to keep from groaning out loud.

After I finished tying Jodi's shoes, she struggled to stand up. I offered her a hand.

"I swear, this baby is bigger than the others," she said, patting her stomach.

I swear, she's going to need a bigger motel room for all these babies.

"Come, on, Benny," I said picking him up off the bed. "Let's go outside and play."

I carried him outside and over to where Rivka was sitting under our usual tree.

Benjamin struggled to get out of my arms, and like a caged animal released to the wild he was off.

"He took a long nap," I informed Rivka, "and now that his battery is fully recharged, Jodi conveniently has a doctor's appointment and we're stuck chasing him around all afternoon. Wanna take bets she planned it this way?"

Benjamin ran over to the sandbox where one of his twin brothers immediately pushed him down.

"Bad, Brian!" he screamed.

"You're a baby!" Brian yelled, before running off.

"I'm not a baby!" Benjamin shrieked after him.

"Benny's a baby! Benny's a baby!" Brian yelled as he ran around the yard.

"I'm not a baby!"

The two of them continued screaming back and forth at each other.

Rivka sat down with her back against a tree. Closing her eyes, she said, "Wake me when all this is over."

I plopped down on the ground next to her. "Oh, no you don't," I said shaking her. "You're not going to La-La Land and leaving me all alone to supervise."

The door on the other side of Jodi's room opened, and Hakeem Jones came out of his room followed by his two little sisters. The girls ran over to the sandbox, and Hakeem came over to us. "Can you watch Trinika and Delilah?" he asked.

"Let me guess. Your mother told you to watch them, and now you're trying to dump them on us," Rivka said.

"I want to go to the clubhouse, and I can't bring them there," he explained.

The clubhouse leans only a few yards away from the Christianson's back steps, too close for our liking from where Rivka and I usually hang out in our *obviously* unsuccessful attempts to hide from babysitter-famished parents. A group of boys at the motel built the clubhouse at the beginning of the summer from a pile of bug-infested lumber they found discarded in the woods. They carted the lumber to the back of the motel, and they spent an entire weekend leaning the boards together and trying to get the pieces to stay upright using Mr. Christianson's hammer and five gallons of nails. When they finally finished their dilapidated monsterpiece, they hung a sign on the door saying, "PRIVAT! NO TRASPAZING!" and even though no female over the age of five would go into that flea-infested crate, they hung another sign below that one which said, "AND NO GURLS NETHER!"

Every boy who lives at the motel who is old enough to break away from his mother hangs out in the clubhouse, and they all think it's the coolest thing they ever crawled into. The gaps between the wood pieces are so wide that when it rains the clubhouse floods inside, and the dirt floor becomes like a puddle of diarrhea, but you think they care? They just bail the water out and then squat in the mud like a pack of piglets.

"Take the girls with you," I said. "They're little enough, and if any of the other boys say anything about it, tell them I told you to."

"Girls aren't allowed," Hakeem said defiantly.

"But they're your sisters," I pointed out.

"Yeah, but they're still girls."

"Sorry, Hakeem. We can't watch them," Rivka said. "We're too busy."

"But you're just sitting here," Hakeem whined.

"Plus, we have too many kids we're watching already," she added.

"So, what's two more?" Hakeem pleaded.

"Nope, sorry. You're going to have to watch them yourself," Rivka said.

Hakeem stomped over to the other side of the yard and flopped down on the ground.

"You know, it really wouldn't be a big deal to watch them since we're stuck here anyway," I said in a low voice.

"I know," Rivka said. "But why should he get to have fun when we can't? Besides, his mother is home. She can watch her own kids just as easily as we could."

The door to the Rivera's room opened and Roberto and Hector came charging out of the room. Their mother followed, dragging her daughter along by the hand.

"YOU TWO STAY IN THE SIDE YARD!" Mrs. Rivera shouted to her sons as she headed towards us.

"Mayday! Mayday!" Rivka whispered.

"Hush, she'll hear you!" I warned.

"Girls, I'm going to the store," Mrs. Rivera announced. "I'll be back soon."

Translation: She'll be gone for at least two hours and we're stuck with her booger-infested brats.

"Be sure to mind Cali and Rivka," she instructed as she nudged Gabby towards the swings.

Rivka started to protest, but Mrs. Rivera was already hurrying towards her car. As soon as her car was out of sight, Roberto took off for the back of the motel with Hector following.

"ROBERTO AND HECTOR GET BACK HERE RIGHT NOW!" Rivka shouted, to no avail.

"That's just great!" I said standing up and debating whether to chase after them. "How are we supposed to watch the Rivera boys if they're out of sight?"

Rivka gave a shrug. "Forget it. I'm not going to worry about them."

"You know we'll be blamed if they get into any trouble," I reminded her.

"Then go drag them out of the clubhouse and make them stay here where we can keep an eye on them."

Rivka sat there daring me to do it, but going to the clubhouse and dragging two boys out of it was even more unappealing than sitting around watching the Hudson boys throw sand at each other.

"Okay...fine!" I said, plopping down on the ground again. "They can stay back there, but if they burn anything down, I'm not paying for it."

Brian Hudson came running over to us. "Andrew won't share the pail and shovel," he sniffled.

"Tell him he'd better or he's going to be locked up in his room by himself," Rivka said.

No sooner had he gone back to his twin brother when the two of them starting screaming and pushing each other around in the sandbox, while the other little kids in the sandbox screamed along with them.

"That's your cue," I said, grabbing the stick she had picked up from the ground out of her hands so she didn't hit anyone with it.

Rivka gave a heavy sigh. "I'm surprised it took this long before the attacks started."

She got up and headed towards the sandbox.

Rivka is the disciplinary member of our babysitting team. She is the one who dishes out threats and breaks up fights, both which involve a lot of yelling. Her talent for yelling at kids was developed after years of listening to her father do the same. I deal more with the after-effects of fights, like the crying when someone gets hurt.

Rivka went over to the sandbox just as one of the twins picked up a handful of sand and threw it at his brother, hitting Rivka instead.

Rivka grabbed each twin by an arm. "That's it!" she yelled. "If you don't behave this second, I'm taking the two of you into the woods and leaving you for the wild coyotes to eat you alive!"

The two boys stopped squirming for an instant and stared at Rivka with their mouths open. Then one of the boys wiggled his way out of Rivka's grasp and ran crying over to Hakeem. The other twin ran over to the patio chair outside his room and there he sat, biting his nails, ready to run inside at the first sign of coyotes. Trinika, Delilah, and Benny sat in the sandbox watching Rivka, their eyes big as saucers.

Rivka came back to where I was sitting. "Well, that settles that," she said sitting down next to me.

I patted her on the back. "I have to admit, Rivka. You really have a way with kids."

Rivka held her head proudly. "Let's hope no one tells them there are no coyotes around here."

Chapter 6

"Who really wears this stuff?" Rivka asked, flipping the pages of an old issue of Teen Fashion Magazine.

It was a rainy Saturday afternoon, and Rivka and I were sitting on the floor in the bathroom of my family's motel room staring at pictures of lamp-post thin models weighing seventy pounds and wearing designer names we've never heard of. As usual, our older sisters Phoenix and Shannon had commandeered the Christianson girls' bedroom, while Pauly and his friends were invading the rest of the Christiansons' apartment. Georgia, Stacey, Isabella Azar, and Gabby Rivera were all playing Chutes and Ladders on one of the beds in our room. On a rainy day, the only place Rivka and I could go for a pea-size amount of privacy was in the bathroom, so that's where we were locked up, planning our social ladder climbing strategy. Of course, by "locked up" I mean we had to sit dead weight in front of the door to keep the younger girls out, because for some stupid reason the motel designers never thought to put a lock on the bathroom door. And privacy? Well...as everyone knows, there's no privacy at this motel. But, at least for the moment, we had a door between us and the younger girls, and we were body blocking it to keep them all out.

"If we want to be one of the Royal Rulers, we need to be more like them," I said.

"How are we going to do that?" Rivka asked, picking at a tiny hole in the knee of her jeans.

"For starters we're going to have to dress more stylish. More like them."

"I don't really like the way they dress," Rivka remarked. "They kind of look slutty."

"I think we're going to have to look a little bit slutty too." I shoved aside some dirty clothes that were on the bathroom floor so I could stretch my legs out.

"I don't want to look slutty," Rivka said.

"Don't you want to be popular?"

"Yes, but do we have to be slutty to be popular?"

"I don't know, Rivka. I'm learning this as we go. I also think it might help some if we worked on your hair."

"No way am I dying my hair magenta."

"No...of course not. I was thinking maybe if you got a hair straightener you could tame some of your curls."

"Who has time to straighten their hair every morning?"

"Do it at night. Stacey could probably help you—she loves that stuff. Maybe it will still be straight enough the next morning."

"I don't want to end up with fried hair from all that heat."

I didn't tell her that her hair already looked fried. "I'm sure they make hair straighteners with some built-in feature so they don't fry hair," I assured her. "And I'm betting your hair would look great straightened."

Rivka jumped up to look at herself in the bathroom mirror.

"Do you really think straightening it would look good?" she asked as she tried to make her curls unroll.

"I really think it would."

"So, what about you?" she asked. "Are you going to straighten your hair every morning too?"

"My hair is already straight."

"You really think straight hair and slutty clothing are the ticket to popularity?"

"And makeup," I added.

"Makeup?"

"Haven't you noticed all the Royal Rulers wear makeup?"

"I always end up looking like a raccoon when I wear makeup," Rivka said.

"Phoenix told me that the trick to wearing makeup is not to rub your eyes once you put it on."

"But, I always rub my eyes."

"Well, if you don't want to look like a raccoon, you have to learn not to."

Rivka looked back at her reflection in the mirror. "I'm really not the makeup-wearing type, Cali."

"If you want to be the popular-girl type, you need to change the way you look. We both do."

Rivka gave a heavy sigh. "Gee, when I was homeschooled, I looked like this and I was tied with Stacey and Shannon for being the most popular girl in school."

"Yeah, it's easy when there are only three girls in the whole school. But, you're in the big leagues now, kiddo, so we've got a lot of work to do to get on Lincoln Middle School's A-list."

All weekend long, the two of us experimented with different wardrobe combinations and practiced putting on some of Phoenix's makeup in an attempt to achieve that stylish look all the Royals had. Monday morning Rivka came out of her apartment dressed in a short skirt, with a long blouse belted at the waist. She was wearing tights and a pair of short black boots. She looked great—except that her mascaraed eyes were already smeared.

"I tried not to rub them, but as soon as I got the mascara on, my eyelashes started to itch."

"You can't scratch them," I said, rubbing the smeared spots off her eyelid as we waited for the bus.

"How can I not scratch an itch?"

"Well, your outfit looks great anyway."

"Thanks, but I've got a bad feeling about this."

"About what?"

"About dressing this way. And if Shannon finds out I took these boots, she's going to cream me."

"Just take them off before you get off the bus this afternoon."

"I'm way ahead of you on that one. I have my sneakers in my backpack so I can change into them on the ride home."

"Well, how about me?" I asked. "How do I look?"

"You look slutty."

"Yeah, that's what Georgia said when she saw me," I said, adjusting my tank top so my bra straps weren't showing so much. "I hope that's good."

When Rivka and I walked into homeroom, heads popped up and eyes followed us as we made our way to our desks. I peeked over at Phoebe to see if she noticed our new look, but she was staring down at her fingernails, watching them grow. I caught sight of Natalie nudging Cassandra and they were both looking at me.

Jake Pellechino leaned over from his desk and said to me, "So, is that your Halloween costume?" I gave him my best Royal shut-your-mouth look.

At lunch Rivka and I ended up with Monica Reilly and Bernice Logan at our table again.

"What's with the outfits?" Monica asked. "They look like something Phoebe would wear."

"Really?" I asked, all dumb-like.

"Yeah, I sort of thought so too," Bernice said. She blew her nose loudly then shoved the used tissue in her lunch bag.

If Bernice and Monica thought our outfits looked like Phoebe's, that must mean we were on the right track. I looked over at Rivka and it took all my willpower not to give her the thumbs up.

Towards the end of lunch period, we noticed Phoebe get up and leave the cafeteria.

"She's probably going to the girls' room," I whispered to Rivka. "Let's go."

"Only one at a time," the lunch monitor told us at the door when we tried to convince her we both really, really needed to go. Toughened up from a thousand years of students trying to play her for stupid, she didn't budge.

"You go," Rivka conceded.

In the girl's room, Phoebe was standing in front of the mirror running her fingers through her magenta hair.

"How's it going?" I asked in a non-caring-kind-of-way since Phoebe always acted like she didn't care too much about anything.

Pretending I didn't care that Phoebe didn't seem to hear me, I started rummaging through my purse for some makeup or a hair brush or anything that would give me a valid reason to stand next to her in front of the mirror. I found a comb and started fussing with my plain old non-magenta hair, in a non-caring-kind-of way, of course.

"You ready for the social studies test?" I asked, trying to sound casual.

Phoebe pushed the sides of her magenta hair away from her face.

"I didn't even study," I babbled on. Of course, it was a lie. I studied for two hours last night, but to admit that would be completely nerdish.

Finally, Phoebe looked over at me, as if she just noticed I was there standing next to her.

"Nice shirt, California Girl." She nodded with approval.

She was out of the girl's room before I recovered enough to say, "Thanks."

Chapter 7

"Not only did Phoebe know my name, but she liked my shirt!" I said to Rivka that afternoon on the back steps. "That must mean we're on the right track."

"Yeah, but everyone else thought our outfits looked ridiculous," Rivka said, taking a sip from her can of soda.

I opened my own can. "No one said we looked ridiculous, did they?"

"No, but they thought it."

"How do you know what they thought?"

"I could see it in their eyes. We looked ridiculous. Slutt-er-ly ridiculous."

"No, we didn't, Rivka. We looked cool."

"If that's cool, I think I'd rather look like a nerd."

Rivka's brother Pauly came over to where we were sitting.

"Roberto won't let me go in the clubhouse," he whined. "He says I smell bad."

"He's right," Rivka said.

"I have no one to play with. Can I stay here with you guys?"

"No, because you smell. Now, get lost," she said.

Normally I would feel bad if I saw someone being mean like that to a little kid, but Pauly isn't just any little kid. He is one of the most annoying kids in the state of New York and Rivka was right to tell him to get lost, especially since he really did smell.

"I'm telling Mommy you won't let me hang out here with you," Pauly said.

"Go right ahead," his sister challenged. "And don't forget to tell her to give you a bath because you smell like a backed-up septic tank."

Rivka took a sip of soda, and just as she did, Pauly reached over and smacked the bottom of the can. The can flew out of her hands, and soda spilled all over her.

"Ha! Ha!" Pauly cried, and took off running.

"You little stink bomb!" Rivka jumped up after him.

Pauly's skinny little legs weren't nearly as fast as Rivka's. She caught him, and wrestled him to the ground where she sat on top of him.

"You apologize, right now, monkey butt!" she yelled in his face.

"MOMMYYYYYYYYY!!!" Pauly screamed at the top of his lungs.

The back door to Rivka's apartment opened up, and Mrs. Christianson's oversized body filled the doorway.

"Rivka!" she yelled, "Get off him this second!"

"He spilled soda all over me!" Rivka yelled back.

"I don't care what he did! You're older and bigger than he is, now get off him."

"Ouch! She's hurting me!" Pauly cried, totally exaggerated of course, but Rivka's mother fell for it.

"Rivka, in the house, now!"

"But, Mom! He started it...."

"NOW!"

Rivka got off Pauly, and as soon as she did, he stuck his tongue out at her. I could tell Rivka wanted to belt him a good one right there, but with her mother watching, it would mean solitary confinement for a year if she tried it.

"Cali, you might as well go on back to your room," Mrs. Christianson said. "Rivka won't be out for the rest of the day."

Drat. That meant we wouldn't be able to coordinate our outfits for school tomorrow.

In our room, Phoenix was sitting on one of the stools at the counter that separated the small kitchenette area from the sleeping area. She was eating a bowl of cereal.

"Is that orange juice in there?" I asked, noticing a yellow tint in her bowl.

"We're out of milk again," she grumbled.

I went to the small refrigerator in the kitchenette and opened it.

"Looks like we're pretty much out of everything," I said.

"Mom didn't get paid yet for the work she did for the newspaper."

Georgia came in from outside.

"What's for supper?" she asked.

I rummaged through the few food items piled on top of the refrigerator. "You can have soup, SpaghettiOs, or cereal with orange juice instead of milk."

"I'll take the soup."

I opened a can of chicken soup, and dumped the contents into two bowls. I heated up Georgia's bowl first in the small microwave on the counter, and when the microwave beeped that it was done, I motioned her over to the empty stool next to Phoenix. Georgia sat down and started eating. After heating up my own bowl, I took it and headed over to the bed to eat.

"You can have my seat," Phoenix said getting up off her stool. "I'm done."

Rarely did all three of us eat a meal together, which was a good thing considering there were only two stools at the kitchenette counter. If more than two people wanted to eat at the same time, whoever got there last usually ended up eating on the bed.

I went and sat next to Georgia to eat my pitiful dinner, which, in all fairness, was better than what Phoenix just finished eating.

"Hey, Phoenix," I said. "Can you help me put together an outfit to wear for school tomorrow?"

"The outfit you have on now looks pretty good."

"Yeah, but I wore it today and I don't have anything else nice for tomorrow."

Phoenix went and opened a drawer to the dresser. "I bought these at the thrift shop the other day. They might be a little bit big on you, but try them on."

She held up a pink V-neck shirt and a beige camisole.

"Really? You'll let me borrow both of them?"

"Yeah, just don't wreck them before I have a chance to wear them."

The shirt was nice enough that no one would guess it came from a thrift store.

"Wow, thanks, Phoenix."

"Maybe after Mom gets paid, we can convince her to take us shopping at the place Mrs. Christianson took me and Shannon. They had some nice things there for pretty cheap."

The next morning, I dressed in a pair of skinny jeans and the shirt and camisole borrowed from Phoenix. Rivka came out of her apartment wearing torn jeans and her paint-splattered sneakers. "Rivka! That is not regal attire!" I cried.

"I decided to go with comfortable," Rivka said.

"And your hair!"

"I didn't have time to straighten it," she said.

"But this is not hair that is going to win you friends." I tried to smooth her hair down, but it kept popping back up.

"If I missed the bus, my dad would end up driving me to school in the Langstermobile," she said. "Or he'd flag down the bus like he did that day when all the younger kids missed it. That would definitely kill any chance of a social life."

I had to agree with her there. Her younger sister Stacey's reputation at school probably is ruined forever thanks to their father. There are about two gajillion kids who live at the motel who go to the local elementary school. Okay, maybe not two gajillion, but around twenty kids. Have you ever seen twenty kids at one bus stop before? The bus picks the kids up at the edge of the parking lot, drives around town picking up more kids, then passes the motel a second time on the other side of Route 9. On the third day of school, the bus came early, and all twenty kids at the motel missed it. The kids were scampering around from room to room at the motel trying to find a parent willing to take them to school, but you know how many parents who live in a motel are willing to drive twenty kids to school? None.

Rivka's father decided to take matters into his own hands. He told all the kids to follow him, and he led them to the end of the motel's parking lot. Then he had them wait on the side of the road while he walked right into the middle of the morning rush hour traffic on Route 9 and held his arms straight out, signaling cars to halt. After all the cars finished slamming on their brakes, the twenty motel kids paraded across to the other side of the road. They waited on the other side of the road until they spotted the bus coming. That's when Mr. Christianson started jumping up and down, yelling in a loud voice, and waving frantically at the bus driver to get him to stop while Rivka's sister Stacey about died from the embarrassment of it. It's bad enough she has to ride the same bus and go to the same school as her brother Pauly, but now she has that history of her dad following her through elementary school too. Embarrassing parental behavior is right up there with throwing up on a teacher, which Pauly ended up doing on the first day of school.

I pulled a container of blush out of my purse. "Rivka, you want to be popular, don't you?" I dabbed a little pink color on her cheeks.

"Yes, but I also want to be comfortable. Can't I be both?"

"No!" Then I gave a sigh. "...I don't know."

That morning before science class started, I finally made contact with Natalie. Not physically like I had the day I slammed into her in the hall, but on a homework level. My desk was right behind Natalie's, which made it very convenient to watch her without her noticing. While the rest of the class was still filing in, I was sitting there noticing how glossy her hair was and wishing my own hair looked that shiny. Suddenly she turned around, and I quickly looked away, hoping she hadn't seen I had been checking out her hair.

She rapped on my desk to get my attention, as if she needed to.

"Hey, you have the homework from last night?" she asked.

"Um...yeah." I nodded.

"Let me copy," she said.

I pulled my homework out of my backpack and handed it to her. She quickly copied my answers.

"Thanks," she said, passing it back.

Score one for the Royal Ruler Wannabe!

Chapter 8

After school that afternoon, Rivka and I were sitting on the back steps behind the motel, thankfully minus Pauly who was now allowed back in the clubhouse after his mother forced him to take a bath the night before.

"Natalie actually asked to copy your homework?" Rivka asked. "The nerve!"

I knew Rivka was right. It takes a lot of guts to ask someone you don't know very well if you could copy their homework, but I also knew if we wanted to be Royals, we had to have nerve too.

"Yeah, it's a little nervy, but it's also a really good thing."

Rivka stared at me in disbelief. "How is that good?"

"Well...now that Natalie knows how nice I am, sharing my homework and all, how could she not want to be friends with us?"

Just then, my mother came around the corner and over to where we were sitting. Her hair was tied back in a ponytail and she was dressed in sweat pants and a tee-shirt—her usual work outfit. Mom was doing some freelance writing to earn a little money until she found a full-time job. She mostly worked out of our room, but occasionally worked at the office of whatever company would hire her. Whenever she had to work in an office, she would transpose herself into a more normal human being, wearing dress slacks and a sweater, but right now she had a big grease stain on her tee-shirt, and she acted like she didn't even care.

"Cali, I'm driving Jodi to the clinic for her checkup," she said. "I told her you'd keep an eye on her boys."

I groaned. "Mommmm! Will you quit volunteering me for babysitting!"

"Jodi needs the help, Cali," my mother said. "Besides, the Hudson boys adore you."

"They don't adore me. They don't even listen to me when I'm watching them."

"You'd be surprised at how much impact you have with them. Now, please go watch them."

"We really need a new hiding place," I muttered to Rivka.

Rivka and I went around to the side yard where the Hudson twins were chasing each other around the yard, screaming like their lungs were about to explode, while Benny sat in the sand box crying.

"Here we go again," Rivka said, plopping down under a tree.

"I guess I should go find out why Benny's crying," I said.

Rivka shook her head. "Whatever it is, he'll get over it. Now explain to me again how doing Natalie's homework for her is helping our quest."

Just then, a door a few doors down from our room opened. Seventeen-year-old Michael Fitzpatrick came out of Room 9 and got into the car parked in front of their room.

"Wow, it's still daylight and MicFitz is actually out of his tomb," Rivka remarked.

"See, I told you he's not a vampire," I said, sitting down on the ground next to her.

"I'm still not convinced," Rivka said. "I mean, he rarely leaves his room and even when he does, he doesn't talk to humans."

"Maybe he's just shy."

Michael slowly backed his parents' car out of its parking spot, somehow avoiding hitting any of the motel kids who didn't have enough sense not to play in parking lot traffic.

"Well, if it's blood he's going out for, I'm sure Phoenix would be happy to donate a few pints," I said as we watched Michael drive away.

My sister Phoenix thinks Michael Fitzpatrick is the most amazing creature alive. She spends most of her free time at the motel trying to get him to notice her, yet Michael doesn't even blink in her 15-year-old direction. Rivka and I can't figure out why Phoenix is madly in love with Michael. As far as we could tell, he's about as dreary and dull as they come.

"I have a feeling your sister won't ever crack the love code on MicFitz," Rivka said.

"I think you're right about that," I admitted.

"And speaking of things I'm right about, I also have a feeling that nothing good will come from doing Natalie's homework."

Now her predictions were back to normal. Shaking my head in disagreement I said, "This will help us break into their circle. This time, I'm the one with a feeling and you should trust me."

Chapter 9

All through September, Rivka and I continued our mission to get in with the popular girls at school. It definitely helped that I sat behind Natalie Picolari in science, and it definitely helped that I did my homework every night and she didn't. After the first time of giving her the answers, Natalie and I got in a routine every morning of me handing her my homework, and her copying the answers onto her paper. In return, Natalie acted not so stuck up towards me. That was definite progress in our popularity climb.

One day in the cafeteria, Rivka and I settled in our usual spot with a clear view of the Royal Rulers' table. We were joined by Monica Reilly and Bernice Logan. We ate our lunch, the whole time pretending we weren't spying on the other table. When Jonathon Parker, Aaron Depasko, and Anthony DeFranco went over to the Royal's table mid-way through the lunch period, Rivka and I were all but taking notes. Apparently, we weren't the only ones.

"I don't get it," Bernice said. "Why do all the boys like them?"

Monica dunked one of her chicken nuggets in barbeque sauce. "They're just sucking up to Phoebe because her mother is famous," she said.

I swiveled around so fast to look at Monica, I nearly popped a neck muscle. "What do you mean Phoebe's mother is famous?"

Monica and Bernice stared at me like I just stepped off an alien craft.

"You don't know who her mother is?" Monica asked.

"Am I supposed to know?" I glanced at Rivka, the so-called psychic, who just shrugged, as clueless as I was.

"Phoebe's mother is Blessing Sheffield!" Bernice exclaimed.

I almost fell out of my chair. "You mean Blessing Sheffield from the movie *Second Generation Truth*?"

Monica nodded. "How many other Blessing Sheffields are there?"

"Seriously?" I looked to see if she was toying with me, but Monica wasn't exactly the toying type.

My mouth was open so wide, I almost drooled. I quickly shut it. "Phoebe is Blessing Sheffield's daughter?"

Monica nodded again. "How did you not know this after being in school with her for almost a month? Haven't you noticed how all the teachers let her get away with everything and the administrative staff practically kisses her feet?"

"I just thought they treated her that way because she's so cool," I said.

Monica shook her head.

"But, why does she go to school here?" Rivka asked. "Don't all celebrity kids go to some big-shot private school?"

"I heard Phoebe refuses to go to some rich girl's school because she says everyone there is stuck up," said Monica. "And the funny thing is she's just as stuck up."

"So, Blessing Sheffield lives right here in Westernton, New York?" I asked, trying to ignore Bernice who was busy blowing her nose hard and loud.

"She used to live here," Monica said, "...before she ran off with her agent."

Throwing her used tissue into her purse, Bernice said, "I overheard Phoebe telling Cassandra that that whole thing was just a publicity stunt her mother and her agent staged."

"If it was just for publicity, why is Phoebe living here with her dad and her grandmother while her mother's in California?" Monica asked.

"I don't know. I'm just telling you what I heard," Bernice said.

Later, on the steps behind the motel, Rivka and I discussed the whole lunch conversation. "Isn't that amazing that her mom's famous?" I asked.

"I think it's kind of sad," said Rivka.

"Sad? Are you kidding! She's so lucky."

"I think it's sad she doesn't live with her mother," Rivka continued. "She probably doesn't get to see her much."

"I don't live with my dad and I haven't seen him in months, but I don't see you getting all pity-like on me."

"I don't know...it just seems worse when it's your mom you don't see. I mean...every kid needs a mom."

"Every kid needs a dad too," I snapped.

Rivka looked surprised. "Wow, I didn't realize not having your dad around was a sore spot for you."

"My dad hasn't called us in months, and you think it doesn't bother me?"

"You never said anything about it before. How was I supposed to know?"

"I never said anything about it because I don't like to talk about it, okay?"

We sat quietly for a few moments, both of us staring at the ground.

Finally, Rivka said, "Sorry, Cali, I didn't mean to sound insensitive."

I shrugged. "I'm sorry I snapped at you. To be honest, I've kind of gotten used to not having my father around, so it's easy not to talk about him."

"Believe me, there are days when I wish my father wasn't around so much," Rivka admitted. "Having your father around all the time is almost as bad as never having him around."

In the case of Mr. Christianson, she was probably right.

"It looks like Phoebe and I have more in common than we thought," I said. "Both of us live in a single-parent home."

"I'm guessing her home isn't anything like yours," Rivka said.

"True, but with us both being products of broken homes, it makes us kindred spirits."

With my newly discovered single-parent connection to Phoebe, I felt even more determined to get into her group. The part about Phoebe's mom being famous made it even more enticing.

Chapter 10

While I was busy sucking up to Natalie in science class by giving her the answers to our homework, I was also working my way onto Phoebe's radar in my math class. My first lucky break came when Mr. Welshire moved Phoebe's seat closer to his desk, and that happened to be right next to mine. I thought it was a lucky break, but the first time I leaned over to ask Phoebe if she wanted to borrow a pencil since she wasn't writing down the homework assignment, Mr. Welshire yelled at us to be quiet. Phoebe who hadn't said a word just rolled her eyes, while Natalie who was sitting on my other side snickered. From that point on I figured Phoebe and I were connected since we got yelled at together, but Phoebe still acted like I didn't exist. When I said 'hi' or 'how's it going' or 'don't you just hate math?' I never got a response from her.

"Tell me again why we want to be friends with them so bad," Rivka said after weeks of homework sharing with Natalie, brown nosing Phoebe, and still no change in our social status.

"We have to be part of the Royal Rulers if we're going to be popular."

"Can't we be popular with everyone but the Royal Rulers?" Rivka asked. "It seems like we're putting in a lot of effort to get in with a group of girls we don't even like all that much."

"I like them," I said.

"I think you like the fact that Phoebe is Blessing Sheffield's daughter."

"Well, I'll admit, that sweetens the deal. But even more than that, it's because for once in my life I want to know what it's like to be popular...to be one of the kids that rule the school instead of being the nerdy, goody-goody kid no one ever notices."

"After watching Natalie and the other girls, I'm not sure being popular is all it's cut out to be," Rivka said.

"What? You don't want to be popular?"

Rivka hesitated a moment. Then she said, "Okay...I'll admit, I wouldn't mind trying it."

But popularity wasn't coming easy for us at Lincoln Middle School. Especially since the most popular girl, Phoebe, acted as if we were invisible. That is, until the day we had a math test on Chapter 3 and Mr. Welshire went out into the hallway to yell at some kids making noise out there.

"Hey, Cali," Natalie whispered loudly. "What's the answers to questions 4, 5, and 8!"

I gave a desperate look towards the door.

"Hurry!" Natalie whispered.

"Number 4 is $x = 32$," I whispered back.

Natalie furiously scribbled on her paper.

"Number 5 the answer is $xy = -42$."

"What?"

"$xy = -42$."

"Here, just write the answers in," Natalie said, passing me her test.

"Natalie...no!" I tried to push it away and looked up just in time to see Mr. Welshire standing in the door watching us.

Natalie snatched her test off my desk.

"She took my test and tried to copy my answers!" she cried to Mr. Welshire when he came over to us.

"*What? No!*" I shook my head furiously at Mr. Welshire.

"I told her I wasn't going to let her cheat off me," Natalie said quickly, "but she grabbed my paper anyway."

"That's not true!"

"Enough!" Mr. Welshire seized both our tests off our desks and ripped them up. "You both get zeros."

It took all my strength not to start crying. I'd never gotten a zero on a test before---ever.

"Time's up!" Mr. Welshire bellowed to those students who didn't have their tests torn up. "Pass your papers forward."

The bell rang, and Natalie pushed her way past me. "Nice going!" she sneered as she went by.

Nice going as in now I have a frickin' zero on a major test? Or *nice going* as in you're a jerk?

"Why were you cheating off of Natalie?" Rivka asked as we walked to my locker after class.

"I wasn't cheating off her! She was cheating off of me!" I said, trying to force the combination on my locker to work. I banged on the metal locker a couple of times, then tried the combination again.

"So, why did you have her test on your desk?" Rivka nudged me aside and opened my locker for me.

I threw my math book inside. "Natalie tried to give me her test to write in the answers for her."

"That's not the way she made it sound—or the way it looked for that matter." Rivka put her math book in my locker too.

"Maybe you're right about her, Rivka. Maybe we need to rethink this getting in with the Royal Rulers just to be popular."

"Yeah, I had a feeling it wasn't going to work out."

In the cafeteria, I went into the sandwich line to buy a tuna wrap, and Rivka went into the hot lunch line to buy chicken nuggets and fries. When I made it through the registers, I didn't see Rivka, so headed over to the table where we usually sat with the other B-listers.

"Hey, California Girl!" Phoebe called from the Royal Rulers' table as I passed by. I pretended not to hear. I was in no mood to listen to her tell me what a pathetic little rodent I was for not grabbing Natalie's test from her hands fast enough.

"Hey, California Girl. Come over here!" My heart skipped a whole measure. I looked over at Phoebe.

"Sit!" she said pointing to the chair next to her.

"*Excuse me?*" I stood there holding my tray not sure if I had heard her right.

"You just gonna stand there with your mouth open, or are you gonna sit with us?" Phoebe asked. Again, she motioned towards the chair next to her, while Natalie sat on her other side with her back turned to us, pretending she didn't care whether or not I sat down. As much as I didn't want to, that's how much I did. I placed my tray on the table and sat down beside Phoebe, hating myself for it and congratulating myself at the same time. Why Phoebe picked today of all days to invite me to sit with them, I wasn't sure.

"Cali?" Rivka came up to the table, and stood there holding her tray.

"What do you want?" Natalie asked, now showing interest in who sat at the table.

Rivka looked at me and seeing as there were no empty seats left, I shrugged not knowing what to do.

Finally, Rivka said, "Um...I guess I'll go sit with Monica and Bernice."

Not knowing what else to say, I said in a small voice, "Okay."

During lunch the Royal Rulers talked mostly about boys. And clothes. And what clothes boys liked girls to wear.

"It was all pretty boring," I said to Rivka later on the back steps when I was telling her about it, trying to downplay it so she didn't feel left out.

"Why did Phoebe invite you to sit with them anyway?" Rivka shuffled the deck of cards in her hands and dealt us each seven cards.

"Either she's taken a liking to me or she felt sorry for me getting a zero." I picked up my cards and looked at them.

"Nice to know she is capable of feeling empathy," Rivka said, rearranging the cards in her hand.

"I don't think she's as bad a person as she pretends to be. It just takes a little work to get to know her."

"Are you going to sit with them tomorrow if they ask you?"

"Are you kidding? Of course, I am!"

Rivka's head shot up from her cards, and she stared at me. "But they cheat off you!"

"But we're practically part of their crowd now."

"Not *we*. You," she pointed out.

"Well, now that I'm sitting with them during lunch, it's only a matter of time before they let you in too."

"Honestly, I don't think I fit in with them."

"Yes, you do, Rivka. At least you will. We both will."

Chapter 11

The next day during math class, Phoebe didn't even look in my direction. Not even when I said hi to her, but Natalie did at least grunt a thank you when I gave her the science homework. At lunch time, I took my tray and told Rivka to follow me. We headed over to the Royal Rulers' table. Phoebe wasn't there, but the others were.

"Mind if we sit with you?" I asked, trying to sound confident, even though I wasn't.

Hailey made a big production of stuffing a forkful of macaroni and cheese into her mouth, making her cheeks puff out more than normal. Cassandra stared down at the food on her tray.

"No room," Natalie finally said, putting her feet up on an empty chair. I looked at another empty chair at their table. "We're saving that," she added.

Rivka stood behind me, and I knew she was thinking what I was thinking; *Now what?*

"Okay. Maybe another time," I said, hoping the flames I felt burning my face weren't showing.

We hurried away towards the table where Monica and Bernice were sitting.

"That was awkward," Rivka whispered.

"They just need more time to get to know us. Once they get to know us, they'll like us."

"I don't think so, Cali. We're too different from them."

The weeks went on, and so did my desire to get in with the Royals. Even though I hated myself for it, I continued to give Natalie the answers in science and other than that, she barely spoke to me. As for Phoebe, after that one day she invited me to eat with them, she didn't acknowledge my existence. When someone doesn't know you're alive, it's hard to try to make small talk. So, I stopped trying.

Then one Friday afternoon at the end of the school day, Rivka and I were heading towards our bus when I heard, "Hey! California Girl! Get over here!"

I looked at Rivka before cautiously walking towards Phoebe and the Royal Rulers. Rivka stayed where she was until I nudged my head for her to follow. I pictured myself bowing and saying something like, *"Yes, Your Royal Highnesses, how can I serve you?"*

"Cassandra has something to ask you," Natalie said when we came up to them.

I turned to Cassandra.

"You're helping Natalie with her science homework, right?" she said.

I nodded.

"Can you also help me...only with math?" she asked.

Considering the zero I had gotten on the math test Natalie had tried to cheat off of no longer made me a candidate for most likely to get an A in math this marking period, I was surprised she even asked. "Um...do you want me to tutor you after school or something?"

"No, just do what you're doing for Natalie. Only instead of science, do the math homework for me. But be sure and make the handwriting look different, okay?"

Hello? What did I look like? Head of the homework cheat ring?

"Oh...and we're all going to the movies tomorrow," she said. "You can come with us if you want."

Whoa! If I want?

I was getting a personal invite to the movies with the Royal Rulers!

Phoebe who had hadn't said anything until that point nodded her head in Rivka's direction. "Goober, you should come too."

Rivka looked annoyed at the nickname, but with her frizzy hair tied in braids, she kind of did look a little Gooberish today.

"So, where do you live?" Cassandra asked.

"What...? Why...?" I stammered.

The girls stared at me like my stupidity mask was on crooked or something.

"We need to know where you live so Cassandra's mother can pick you up," Natalie said.

"Yeah, my mom's picking everyone up around 12:30," Cassandra said. "I guess she can give you a ride too."

The excitement of being invited to go with them was taken over by a feeling of panic.

"Actually...we don't need a ride," I said. "I'll just have my Mom drop me and Rivka off at the theater because we have to go somewhere tomorrow morning anyway."

"Oh? Where you going?" Cassandra asked.

"Um...shoe shopping," I said.

"Shoe shopping?" Natalie questioned.

"New shoes," I tried to explain. "For school. I mean, look at these!"

Everyone looked down at my shoes.

"O.M.G.," Natalie said. "You sure do need new shoes."

Great! Now I had to figure out a way to get new shoes by tomorrow afternoon.

"So, we don't need a ride," I said, trying to distract everyone from scrutinizing my shoes any longer.

"Fine, whatever," Natalie said. "We'll be at the 1:00 show at the Clearview Cinemas."

"Do you want my mom to give you a ride home after the movie?" Cassandra asked.

"NO!" Rivka and I practically shouted at the same time.

"We don't need a ride," I said. "Rivka's mom drives by the cinemas all the time, doesn't she, Rivka?"

"Yeah, all the time," Rivka nodded frantically.

"She can give us a ride home, so don't worry about us," I said.

Before they had a chance to say anything else, I said to Rivka "We better hurry before the bus leaves." I grabbed her hand and we flew towards our bus.

"So, now you have to do Cassandra's homework for her too?" Rivka asked when we were settled in our seats on the bus.

"Yeah, but they invited us to go to the movies with them. Did you not hear that part?"

"Of course, I heard. But how are we going to get there? Our parents won't want to drive us. And where are we going to get the money to go?"

"Don't worry. We'll figure something out," I said.

"And where did you come up with shoe shopping?" she giggled.

"I don't know! It just came out! I hope Phoenix has some shoes I can borrow for tomorrow," I said. "I can't be seen wearing these, that's for sure."

"We forgot to ask what movie we're going to see," Rivka said.

"Does it matter? We got invited to go to the movies with the most popular girls at Lincoln Middle School."

We high-fived each other.

When the bus dropped us off at the motel, Rivka followed me to my room. Mom was sitting on the bed, hunched over her laptop, a bag of chips next to her. She didn't even look up when we came in.

"Mom, Rivka and I need a ride to the movies tomorrow afternoon."

"What time?" she asked clicking away at the keys.

"Around 12:30."

"I guess. How are you getting home?"

"Can you pick us up after?"

"Nope. I have a writer's group meeting in Cambridge at 1:30. I'm not sure when I'll be back." She grabbed a handful of chips and shoved them in her mouth without taking her eyes off the screen.

"Maybe my mom can bring us home," Rivka said.

Rivka and I went to the Christiansons' apartment and found her mother in the girls' bedroom changing sheets.

"Can't," Mrs. Christianson said when Rivka asked for a ride home. "Tomorrow I'm meeting up with my old friend, Mary Marchand. She'll be here this weekend on business and wants to get together."

"Can't you pick us up first before you meet up with her?" Rivka begged. "We got invited to go to the movies with the most popular girls at school, so this is really important."

"Maybe one of their parents can drive you home after the movie," Mrs. Christianson suggested.

"No!" we both answered at once.

"Well...go ask your father then," Mrs. Christianson said.

"Not Dad!" Rivka moaned. "You know how he embarrasses us every time he opens his loud mouth."

"I'm sorry, Rivka. If your father can't pick you up, then I guess you'll just have to go another time."

Desperate, we went off to look for Mr. Christianson. We found him under the Christiansons' kitchen sink. Or at least we found the bottom half of him. We couldn't really see his top half because it was inside the cabinet under the sink.

"Dad, Cali and I need a ride home from the Clearview Cinemas tomorrow," Rivka said to the legs sticking out from the cabinet.

"WHAT?" he yelled. "I CAN'T HEAR YOU!"

Rivka scooted down to talk into the cabinet. "Can you pick us up at the movies tomorrow around 3:30?"

"I GUESS SO. HAND ME THAT WRENCH!"

Rivka handed him a wrench that was lying on the floor beside her.

"We need to be picked up at the Clearview Cinemas. The place near Costco."

"YUP, I KNOW THE PLACE...OH, FOR CRIPES SAKES, THIS THING'S STILL LEAKING!"

"Now Dad, don't you dare pick us up in the Langstermoble," Rivka warned.

"YEAH, YEAH...OH CRAP!" A loud string of swears came from under the sink.

"Did you hear me, Dad?" Rivka said louder. "NO LANGSTERMOBILE!"

"GOTCHA! HAND ME THAT DUCT TAPE," he yelled from under the sink.

Rivka said to me, "We are so dead!"

Chapter 12

The next day, Rivka and I were in her bedroom getting ready for the movies. Rivka was wearing a white hoody and distressed jeans with tears at the knees that were in style back in the '90s. The sad thing about it was that her jeans weren't purposely ripped to be stylish. They got that way from wrestling her brother on the ground so often. I was wearing a denim mini skirt and a cute top Mrs. Christianson had bought at the thrift store for Rivka, but Rivka didn't like it, so I inherited it. On my feet, I wore a pair of black flats which Rivka's sister Shannon was nice enough to loan me after my own sister flat out refused to let me borrow a pair of her shoes because she was worried I'd get them all sticky on the bottom at the movie theater. Shannon was also nice enough to loan both me and Rivka the money to pay for the movie, because unlike those of us who watch children around the motel (for free!), she actually gets paid for pet sitting dogs, cats, and other assorted critters for people who live in the wealthier part of town.

After I finished putting on some makeup, Rivka looked at me funny.

"Too much?" I asked.

"A little."

I wiped off some of the blush and lipstick.

"Maybe you should put a little more on," I said.

"Where does it say you have to wear makeup to be popular?" Rivka said.

"Nowhere. It's just popular people always look fashionable, and makeup helps."

"When I'm Queen, I'm going to change all the rules," Rivka said. "The natural look and comfy clothes will be the thing to wear."

"Did you remind your father to meet us around the corner from the movies and not in the parking lot?" I asked her.

"Yeah, but at the time he was fixing one of the washers in the laundry room so there is no guarantee the message sunk in."

Knowing Mr. Christianson, he probably already forgot that Rivka had pleaded with him not to pick us up in the Langstermobile, and I was nervous about it. It would not help our case if the Royal Rulers caught a glimpse of us getting into that vehicle.

My mother dropped us off at the cinemas early and we waited in the lobby for the other girls to show up.

Phoebe walked in first, followed by Natalie, Cassandra, and Hailey.

"Those your new shoes?" Natalie asked looking down at my feet. "They looked used."

"I couldn't find anything I liked at the store," I lied. "These are an old pair."

Natalie glanced at Rivka's paint-splattered sneakers. "It wouldn't hurt you to buy some new shoes yourself," she said.

Everyone looked at Rivka's feet.

"I think Goober's shoes have character," Phoebe commented.

Natalie and Cassandra exchanged disbelieving looks. Rivka and I did the same.

"What movie are we seeing?" I asked, once again trying to walk the topic away from shoes.

"We should go see your mom's new movie!" Hailey squealed to Phoebe. Phoebe didn't bother answering her. Instead, she went to the ticket window and bought a ticket for a movie her mother wasn't in, *The Seventh Sacred Heart*. We all copied her.

Inside the theater, Cassandra, Natalie, and Hailey jostled each other trying to sit next to Phoebe. Natalie won one side, and Cassandra ended up on the other. I sat next to a pouting Hailey, and Rivka was next to me on the end. During the movie, Cassandra kept whispering stuff to Phoebe and giggling. Natalie kept leaning over Phoebe and telling Cassandra to shut up. About halfway through the movie, Phoebe had enough of both of them, climbed over the back of her seat, and sat in the row behind us by herself. Without moving our heads, Rivka and I tried to make eye contact with each other to see what the other thought, but afraid Phoebe might be watching us from behind, we dared not look directly at each other.

When the movie ended, Phoebe didn't bother waiting for any of us, and was already up the aisle before we even turned around. Natalie rushed after her and the rest of us followed.

The bright sunshine slammed into our eyes as we came out of the theater.

"I don't see my mom yet," Cassandra said, scanning the parking lot.

Rivka and I also scrutinized the parking lot, hoping Rivka's father remembered to meet us around the corner. We didn't see the bright red Langstermobile, but instead, spotted a blue Toyota with Michael Fitzpatrick leaning against it. He raised his hand ever so slightly to wave at us.

"What's MicFitz doing here?" I whispered to the psychic Rivka, who shrugged, just as confused as I was.

"*Who is that?*" Natalie asked us, catching the quick wave.

"That's...um...Michael," I answered, not sure if he was here for us, or if he was waiting for someone else.

Phoebe nodded her approval. "Not bad," she said.

"Yummy!" Natalie added, her eager eyes staring intently in Michael's direction.

"He...he's a *really* good friend," I said. I looked at Michael with new eyes, and realized he actually wasn't that bad looking. Suddenly, the person Rivka and I had pegged as being dreary and dull was a hot commodity in our effort to get on the A-list.

We walked over to the Toyota with Natalie, Cassandra, and Hailey following. Phoebe stayed standing against the building, watching. The three Royals were giggling and nudging each other out of the way to get a better view of Michael...or should I say, to let him get a better view of them.

"Your dad was busy," Michael said to Rivka. "He asked me to pick you up."

It was the most I ever heard him say in one sentence. Or in one day, even.

"I'm Natalie," Natalie said pushing past the other girls to get closer to Michael. "I'm 15 years old."

Whoa! Major lie. She couldn't be more than 13.

"I had a late birthday that's why I'm not in high school yet."

Michael shrugged, then said to Rivka and me, "Ready?"

I gave a quick wave to Phoebe who was still standing by the building, and said to the other Royal Rulers, "Thanks for letting us come with you today. See you in school on Monday."

Natalie, Cassandra, and Hailey were so busy trying to show off for Michael, I don't think they heard me. Looks like Phoenix wasn't the only one who thought Michael was some kind of luscious dessert from the gods. When Michael got into the car, Rivka and I both tried to get in the front passenger seat at the same time. Rivka, being in better shape from daily wrestling with her brother, managed to body block me and won. Defeated, I got into the back seat by myself.

As we drove away, I glanced out the window, and I swear I saw Natalie throw a kiss in our direction.

The inside of the Fitzpatricks' car was immaculately clean and smelled like a forest, thanks to the cardboard pine tree that hung from the rearview mirror. We rode in silence for a while until finally Rivka said to Michael, "Thanks for coming to pick us up. You probably saved our lives."

"Yeah, thanks," I added.

Michael didn't respond. He just stared at the road ahead.

"We were worried my dad was going to show up in the Langstermobile," Rivka continued.

When Michael still didn't say anything, I added, "Yeah, that would have been a social catastrophe for us."

Michael kept driving, and Rivka turned and gave me a single raised eyebrow, which meant she didn't think Michael fully understood the whole being seen in the Langstermobile thing. I mean, how could he understand? His mother and father are practically normal as far as parents go. They're polite, they don't dress in embarrassing clothing, and they don't yell in public. What kid wouldn't want parents like that?

We rode in silence until we were nearly to the motel. When Michael finally spoke, Rivka and I both jumped in surprise.

"One time, my mother drove me to school wearing her robe and slippers, and when I left my lunch on the seat of the car, she came into the school to give it to me dressed like that."

"No way!" I breathed.

"Man, that's cruel," Rivka said.

Michael nodded. "I wanted to die that day."

Okay, so maybe we all have our embarrassing moments with our parents.

As we drove into the parking lot of the motel, we saw Phoenix sitting on the curb outside our room. When she spotted me and Rivka getting out of the car with Michael, she nearly choked on her own drool.

"Thanks for the ride, Michael," I cooed, trying to sound sexy for Phoenix's benefit, not Michael's.

"Yeah, thanks," Rivka said. "You really saved us a world of embarrassment not having my dad pick us up."

"Anytime," Michael said. He went in his room and shut the door without even looking in Phoenix's direction.

I couldn't help but give Phoenix a gloating smile as Rivka and I headed to the back steps to talk things over. Phoenix jumped up and followed us.

"You got to ride with Michael?"

"Yup, and he's so majorly hot!" I faked the love.

"Cali, he's mine, so don't even go there!" Phoenix warned.

"Really? Well, who's the one he gave a ride to?"

Okay, I was gloating way more than I should, considering I didn't even like him that way, but I was still mad at her for not letting me borrow her shoes to go to the movies.

"So, what did he say?" Phoenix asked, following behind us as we walked. "Did he talk to you on the ride?"

"Are you kidding? We could hardly get him to shut up." I looked over at Rivka and she bit down on her lip to keep from laughing.

Phoenix stayed on our heels. "What did he talk about? Did he ask about me?"

"Nope. Later. Come on Rivka." We picked up our pace hoping Phoenix got the message we didn't want her with us. She did.

"So...what did you think of them?" I asked as we plopped down on the back steps.

"Who?"

"The Royal Rulers."

"They don't seem to like each other very much," Rivka answered.

"Sure, they do. Why else would they go to the movies together? And eat lunch together every day?"

"I don't know...I didn't get a warm, fuzzy feeling being with them."

"But they're the most popular girls in school!"

"I'm just saying...I didn't feel very comfortable being with them."

"Well, get used to it, Rivka. This is the group we belong in if we want to be popular."

"Well, then get used to doing all their homework for them," Rivka said, "because I think that's the only reason they're letting us in their group."

Chapter 13

October brought in several days of unseasonably warm weather that felt like summer again. Rivka and I were sitting on the grass in the playground area, keeping one eye on the Jones girls and the other on Old Man Malcolm who was sitting in front of his room salivating at all the young, tender prey darting around in front of him.

In addition to all the families living at the motel, there's this one old guy, Old Man Malcolm, who spends all his time parked in the chair in front of his room watching everything that goes on around the motel. Rivka and I think maybe he's a serial killer waiting for the right moment to lure unsuspecting victims into his room so he could snuff their lives out with a motel room pillow. Mom says he's just a lonely old man whose only source of entertainment is people watching.

"Why don't we take all the kids over to him and let him have his pick," Rivka suggested, drawing an O in the dirt with a stick.

"Did your dad ever do a background check on him?" I asked, taking the stick from her and placing an X in the bottom right-hand corner of the tic-tac-toe board we had drawn in the dirt.

"Nah, he doesn't do that sort of thing," Rivka said, taking the stick from me and drawing another O in the dirt.

"Yeah, I guess if he did, none of the people living here would pass inspection."

Suddenly, the Hudson twins Andrew and Brian came running out of their room.

"HELP! SOMEBODY, HELP!" Andrew yelled.

"What's the matter now?" Rivka called over to him.

"THE BABY'S COMING!" Brian screamed.

"Did he just say what I think he said?" Rivka asked me.

"THE BABY'S COMING!" both twins screamed at the same time.

Instantly, motel doors flew open everywhere.

The twin boys kept jumping up and down screaming, "THE BABY'S COMING!" as people came out of their rooms and hurried over towards them.

Rivka and I each grabbed one of the Jones girls and ran over to where everyone was congregating outside Jodi's room. Inside, Jodi was curled up on her bed moaning. Two-year-old Benjamin was sitting next to her crying. Mom, Mrs. Jones, Mrs. Rivera, and Mrs. Christianson, who had all come running from out of the office, pushed their way through the crowd and went inside. Mrs. Jones picked Benjamin up off Jodi's bed and hugged him close. "Don't y'all worry, Sugar. Your mama's fine," she cooed to him. "Your mama's goin' to be just fine."

Benny stopped crying, mesmerized by all the pink and purple fur growing out of Mrs. Jones' hat.

"Rivka!" Mrs. Christianson yelled. "Tell your father to bring the car around!"

Rivka put down Trinika who she was holding, and dashed behind the back of the motel.

"Now everyone's in my way!" Trinika started whining. "I want to see the baby."

"The baby's not here yet," I told her. "Jodi has to go to the hospital first."

Mom, Mrs. Rivera, and Mrs. Christianson were coaching Jodi to take deep breaths, but Jodi wasn't taking directions very well and just moaned louder.

It wasn't long before Mr. Christianson came zooming around from the back of the motel, not with the Christiansons' beige Honda, but with the red Langstermobile. He pulled up as close to Jodi's room as the crowd allowed.

"LET 'EM THROUGH!" Mr. Christianson yelled out the window as his wife and my mother came out of the room supporting Jodi between them. Mrs. Rivera was walking behind them, her arms outstretched in case Jodi decided to faint or drop a baby or something. Even wearing high heels Mrs. Rivera was smaller than me, so if it came right down to it, she'd be blown over if she even caught a breeze as Jodi went down.

"Don't you worry about anything, *Hunny*," Mrs. Jones said to Jodi. "W'all take good care of your l'il sugar pies while *yewr* in the hospital."

Jodi's eyes looked scared and grateful at the same time. She was about to say something, but instead let out a cry that sounded like the baby was pressing down on her vocal cords.

Mom and Mrs. Christianson eased Jodi into the back of the Langstermobile before getting in themselves. With a loud screech of tires, Mr. Christianson took off out of the parking lot for the hospital. The sign on the top of the van was lit up inviting people to stay at Langster Motel.

"Well, I hope for the baby's sake Jodi doesn't give birth in the Langstermobile," Rivka said. "There is no hope for a normal life for any kid born in the back seat of that thing."

The next few hours dragged by, waiting to hear about the baby. Everyone hung around in the parking lot, the side yard, or sat outside their rooms waiting for some kind of news. Shannon and Phoenix sat outside the office door listening for the phone, and when it rang, they both jumped up and ran inside. When they came back out, Shannon shouted to everyone that Mrs. Christianson had called to say Jodi gave birth to a seven-pound baby girl. A loud cheer went up around the parking lot. Little kids started jumping up and down in excitement.

Mrs. Jones was sitting in a chair outside her room with her daughter Trinika on one knee and Benjamin Hudson on her other. "What's the baby's name?" she called over to Shannon.

"Langster!" Shannon yelled back.

Everyone in the parking lot went quiet for a moment and just stared at Shannon and Phoenix in disbelief.

"Are you serious?" Rivka asked.

"No way!" I insisted.

Shannon was deadpan for a moment before she and Phoenix burst out laughing.

"Just kidding!" Shannon snorted. "Jodi named the baby Juliana."

A relieved chuckle trickled through the group, then everyone dispersed back to their rooms.

It was a couple of days before Jodi came home from the hospital with Juliana. While she was gone, little Benny stayed with the Jones in their room since Mrs. Jones had a way of calming him that no one else did. I found it amazing that one of the moms who rarely had time to watch her own kids took in one more kid that she could dump on Rivka and me to watch. The Hudson twins stayed with the Christiansons and shared the pull-out sofa bed in the living room with Pauly. And of course, Rivka and I were forced to watch all three of the Hudson boys whenever we weren't in school or using the bathroom for two minutes—which was about the only amount of time we are allowed for bathroom breaks—so that the adults could maintain their childless lives.

The day Jodi came home with Baby Juliana, the entire motel population met them in the parking lot.

The motel moms made such a fuss over the new baby you'd think they never had kids of their own—which I suppose was easy to forget since their own kids were always in Rivka's and my care.

"Wow, look at all that hair she has," Mrs. Christianson remarked.

Mrs. Fitzpatrick said, "Look how perfectly round her head is."

"What a darlin' peach she is," Mrs. Jones said, touching the baby's cheeks to check for ripeness.

Okay, I'll admit it, the baby was kind of cute, but if there was one thing this motel didn't need, it was one more kid. I'm no psychic like some people around here, but even I could predict Rivka and I would be babysitting her within a week.

Chapter 14

After school one afternoon, Rivka and I were sitting on the ground next to the maple tree, a pile of crunchy scarlet leaves under us, and a sleeping newborn baby in a carrier next to us. Mom had taken Jodi for a follow-up visit to her doctor, and lucky girls that we were, Rivka and I got to watch all four of the Hudson kids while they were gone. Lucky, as in *yeah, right*!

"Halloween is only a week away," Rivka commented as she drew brown pumpkins in the dirt with a stick. "My parents figured instead of having the kids go trick-or-treating room to room this year, we'd have a party that everyone can go to."

"Do kids actually go trick-or-treating room to room?" I asked.

"Last year they did. Where else would they go around here?"

"I just assumed everyone would go trick-or-treating in the wealthier areas, like near where your sister pet sits."

"Parents aren't going to want to drive their kids anywhere. My parents thought instead of trick-or-treating we could hold a party in the rec room."

The rec room is a separate one-room building located around the back of the motel.

When we first arrived and heard there was a special room for recreational activities, Phoenix, Georgia, and I visualized things like video game systems set up in there, maybe a pool table, a pinball machine, anything that might be remotely fun, but it was a huge disappointment to discover the room had nothing but tables and chairs in it.

"Dad said he'll buy pizza out of the motel petty cash fund, and Mom's going to check with the other parents to see who else can contribute food or candy."

"Do we have to go?" I asked.

"Why? You don't want to?"

"Think about how many parents will dump their kids off in the rec room and make us watch them while they go somewhere else."

"Good point," Rivka agreed. "Maybe we can dress up so no one recognizes us."

"How are we going to get costumes without any money?"

"We'll just go as something easy. Like a ghost."

"Boring."

"Or a bum."

I glanced at her torn jeans. "No stretch there."

"Okay, forget the bum. How about conjoined twins?"

"Conjoined twins?"

"It's an easy-enough costume. We could borrow some clothes from my Uncle Stanley who lives in Ridgefield. He's so big, we could both fit into a pair of his pants."

"Isn't that disrespectful?"

"What? Wearing a fat person's clothes?"

"Going as conjoined twins."

"It's a costume party, Cali. Half the Halloween costumes of the world aren't respectful."

Disrespectful or not, Rivka called her uncle to ask if we could borrow one of his shirts and a pair of his pants, and a few days later Uncle Stanley Christianson came by the motel with an extra set of clothing for us.

Before the party started on Halloween, I met Rivka at her apartment, and we spent the next fifteen minutes in her bedroom trying to figure out how to conjoin ourselves. First, Rivka put both her legs in one leg of Uncle Stanley's pants. I climbed into the other pant leg. Then we each placed one of our arms in a sleeve of Uncle Stanley's shirt and our arms that were closest to each other we placed around each other's back, hidden inside the shirt. Buttoning up the shirt took us awhile, but working together with our free hands, we managed to do it. It actually was an easy Halloween costume. Easy, that is, until we tried walking. Our legs were pressed together so tightly in our individual pant leg that the only way to walk was by taking itty, bitty baby steps or by hopping with both feet. First, Rivka and I tried the baby steps method, but we didn't get very far that way. Next, we tried hopping together at the same time, but we found if we got out of sync, we'd lose our balance and nearly topple over. We finally coordinated our hops so she would take one hop first, then I'd hop. She'd hop. I'd hop. We started a Dr. Seuss chant as we practiced—*One hop, two hop, red hop, blue hop.* Once we got our rhythm down, we hopped on over to the motel's rec room.

"HECTOR! GET OFF OF THERE!" Mrs. Rivera was yelling, as we hopped into the room.

Hector, dressed as a superhero of some kind with a blue cape made from a towel, took a flying leap off the top of a banquet table, then took off running away from his mother.

Rivka's brother Pauly was chasing after a silver-clad Reza Azar screaming, "I'm going to suck your brains out!"

Pauly was dressed as a zombie with hideous lipstick blood smeared all over him. A handful of costumed characters were chasing each other in circles and laughing in high-pitched screeches. It seemed everyone under the age of ten was running around the room screaming their Halloween-costumed heads off.

Over in one corner, Mr. Christianson was setting up a microphone and some speakers. *"TESTING! TESTING!"* he yelled into the microphone. His booming voice was magnified ten times louder than normal.

Georgia and Stacey dressed as angels with halos made from coat hangers wrapped with silver Christmas garland were twirling around in the center of the room. Isabella Azar dressed as a princess was watching them, too shy to join in.

Jodi's three boys were all dressed as ghosts, and from the looks of their costumes, I'm pretty sure Jodi cut up a couple of motel sheets to make them. You can bet when Rivka's father notices, there will be some major yelling taking place, more so than normal. Jodi was sitting in a chair with one ghost on her lap and another hanging on the back of her chair. A third ghost was running around the chair, stopping occasionally to scream

"*BOO!*" in his mother's face. Baby Juliana was in a carrier on the floor next to Jodi's chair, and I figured it was only a matter of time before the hyperactive ghost running in circles tripped over her.

Near the bean bag toss were half a dozen kids waiting their turn to throw a bean bag through a hole in a wooden board. Hakeem "the Jedi" Jones was standing in line waving his light saber in the air and shouting, "MAY THE FORCE BE WITH YOU!"

When we hopped past them, Hakeem asked, "What are you supposed to be?"

"We're conjoined twins," Rivka said.

"What's conjoined twins?" asked Delilah Jones Square Pants.

"It's twins whose body parts are connected," I explained.

"So, you're like a two-headed monster?" asked Roberto Rivera, who had a plastic axe attached to his head, and fake blood coming down his face.

"No, we're not a two-headed monster," Rivka said. "We're twins who were joined together at birth with two hands, two feet, and two heads, but only one body."

"Like a two-headed monster," said Roberto.

"The only monster I see is standing right in front of us, and he only has one head," Rivka huffed. "Come on, Cali. Let's get something to eat."

We hopped over to the table where Mrs. Rivera, Mrs. Christianson, and Mrs. Azar were passing out slices of pizza, orange frosted cupcakes, and apple cider.

Mrs. Azar and her husband, along with their daughter and son, Isabella and Reza, live in Room 8. Her English isn't too good, and I'm not sure Mr. Azar even knows English because he never talks.

"Ahhh...*look* how cute you *goouls* are!" said Mrs. Azar.

"Yes, wasn't that a clever idea they came up with, going as Siamese twins?" Mrs. Christianson said, looking at us proudly.

"They no look like twin Siamese cats to me," Mrs. Azar said.

Mrs. Christianson and Mrs. Rivera burst out laughing.

"No...not Siamese cats--they're Siamese twins," Mrs. Christianson explained.

"Mom, we're *conjoined* twins!" Rivka corrected. "No one uses the term Siamese twins anymore."

"Conjoined? What is conjoined?" Mrs. Azar asked, looking confused at an unknown English word.

Mrs. Christianson and Mrs. Rivera tried to explain to Mrs. Azar what conjoined twins were, but Rivka cut them off.

"We're two people with one body," she said.

Mrs. Azar laughed. "Ooooh!! Ha! Ha! Two-people body. How cute!"

Just then, Roberto ran by the refreshment table. Mrs. Rivera yelled after him, "ROBERTO, WHAT DID YOU DO NOW?"

Roberto kept running and yelled behind him, "I DIDN'T DO ANYTHING, MA!"

Hector came running behind his big brother and cried, "I DIDN'T DO ANYTHING NEITHER!"

We looked over at a group of girls and saw Roberto's sister Gabby crying, while Georgia and Stacey tried to comfort her.

"Oh, those boys!" Mrs. Rivera exclaimed, heading over to her daughter to find out what damage her brothers had done to her this time.

Even with all the clamor in the room, you could still hear Mrs. Rivera's high heels clacking noisily as she made her way across the room.

Rivka and I grabbed slices of pizza from the refreshment table, and with only one free hand each, tried to figure out the best way to eat them. Neither of us had ever tried to eat pizza with one hand before, and quickly found out it was impossible. Giving up on the pizza in order to save poor Uncle Stanley's clothes from further pizza sauce stains, we wolfed down some cupcakes and then bunny hopped over to the karaoke corner, where Phoenix was going through some CDs.

"Anything good?" I asked.

"No, it's all oldies," Phoenix grumbled. "Like from five years ago."

Not having any good songs to sing was a small relief. That would mean Phoenix wouldn't sing karaoke. Not that she was a bad singer or anything—she actually was pretty decent. It's just every time people heard her sing, they assumed I was a good singer too. Unfortunately, I have a singing voice like a frog with marbles in his mouth, but that didn't stop people from trying to get me to sing anyway. Especially during karaoke.

Rivka rifled through the CDs. "Oh, my gosh! This is perfect!" she said pulling one out. "Let's sing *Double Danger Girls*, Cali!" Rivka said. "Wouldn't that be hysterical?"

"Um...no?"

"Oh, come on. We totally should."

"I don't do karaoke, Rivka. And since you and I are attached together for the evening, you're not doing karaoke tonight either."

Shannon Christianson came over with a handful of Tootsie Rolls. She handed Phoenix half of the candy and kept the other half. "Awww...look at you all dressed up like the little kids," she said to her sister, as she unpeeled a Tootsie Roll.

"Well, look at you with that scary face even without a Halloween mask," Rivka retorted back, trying to snatch a Tootsie Roll out of her hand.

You could easily see that Shannon and Rivka were sisters, but Shannon is a much softer, prettier version. Her blond hair always looks stylish instead of like a bird's nest like Rivka's. Shannon has freckles too, but only a small sprinkle of them, not splattered everywhere like Rivka's. I think Rivka is jealous of her sister's looks, but maybe I just think that because my own sister Phoenix is tons prettier than both me and Georgia put together, and I can't help but feel jealous.

"Fitzpatrick alert!" cried Phoenix, seeing Mr. and Mrs. Fitzpatrick walking into the rec room.

My sister quickly smoothed down her auburn hair, pinched her cheeks, and bit her lips.

"How do I look?" she asked Shannon.

"Great," Shannon replied, "but I don't see Michael with them."

Michael's father headed over to help Mr. Christianson who was swearing at the speakers that refused to work properly. Mrs. Fitzpatrick came over to us.

"Hi, girls," she said with a smile. She was slim and dressed in black slacks and a white sweater. Her neatly combed hair was just starting to show signs of gray.

"Is Michael coming?" Phoenix asked her, looking at the door in hopes of seeing her main crush walk through it.

"He's back at the room doing homework," Mrs. Fitzpatrick said.

Phoenix made a face. "Homework? On Halloween?"

Mrs. Fitzpatrick nodded. "I'm afraid that boy spends entirely too much time holed up in our room."

"I'll say!" Phoenix agreed.

"He's so busy doing homework all the time, he probably doesn't even have a clue that a certain someone is all ga-ga over him," Shannon added.

Phoenix jabbed her with her elbow.

"Maybe you girls could try to convince him to come to the party for a little while," Mrs. Fitzpatrick suggested.

"Sure, we'll give it a try. Come on, Shannon!" Phoenix grabbed Shannon's arm and practically dragged her out of the room.

"IS THIS THING WORKING NOW," Mr. Christianson yelled into the microphone. The adults jumped in surprise from the volume, and the young kids covered their ears in pain. Obviously, it was working.

Rivka and I hopped over to the other side of the room where some folding chairs were set up. We moved two chairs close together and on the count of three, we both parked our butts down. Like everything else we did as conjoined twins, sitting required coordination.

A few moments later we saw Phoenix and Shannon come back without Michael.

"I guess they couldn't convince MicFitz being with them was more fun than doing homework," Rivka said.

"Why are the Fitzpatricks living here anyway?" I asked. "Based on their nice clothing and their new car, I'm guessing they aren't government-assistance recipients like everyone else around here."

"My mother said Mr. Fitzpatrick lost his job last year, and they ended up having to sell their house a few months ago because they couldn't afford it anymore."

"So, why didn't they just move into an apartment, or at least stay at a better motel than this one?"

"I don't know why they chose this place, but they're waiting until Mr. Fitzpatrick finds work before they rent a place because they don't want to move again if he gets a job in another state."

Mrs. Azar walked by our chairs with a bowl of Halloween candy. "You two-headed *goouls* not playing with the other kiddies?" she said holding out the bowl.

Rivka and I both took a handful of candy from it.

"We're too old to play," Rivka said, biting into a piece of licorice.

"Especially with these kids," I added, trying to unpeel a Tootsie Roll with my teeth and my one free hand.

"Ah...but not too old for kiddie candy," Mrs. Azar said.

"You're never too old for candy," I informed her.

"Ha! Ha! You fairy funny *goouls*," she said walking away.

"What's so funny about not being too old for candy?" I asked Rivka.

"Not a thing," Rivka replied. "But Mrs. Azar is a funny little lady."

"Okay!" Rivka's father yelled into the microphone—not that he needed a microphone to be heard, mind you. "Everyone with a costume form a circle in the middle of the room! We're going to pick the best costume and the winner gets this giant elephant balloon."

He held up a pink blow-up elephant on a stick and a collective shriek went up from the little kids in the room. A few adults groaned. Who could blame them for not wanting a giant blow-up elephant in a motel room already at maximum junk capacity?

Even though winning the elephant balloon was even dumber than winning a pack of gum in a scavenger hunt, Rivka and I decided we'd try to win it anyway. We hopped to the circle of costumed kids that was forming in the middle of the room. Our heads towered over everyone else's.

Roberto pushed his way into the circle of kids.

"Hey, quit pushing me!" Pauly whined.

"ROBERTO!" Mrs. Rivera yelled.

"I didn't do anything, Ma!" Roberto yelled back.

"Me neither!" Hector automatically yelled from the other side of the room.

When the circle, or something that looked like one, was finally filled with costumed kids, Mr. Christianson waved his hands over the noise to get everyone's attention.

"Okay, when the music starts, I want you to parade around in the circle so all the adults can see your costume," he hollered.

"But Daddy, everyone can already see our costume now. Why do we have to walk in a circle for them to see?" Stacey asked.

"Just parade, Stacey! Parade!" her father ordered.

He pressed the button on the CD player, and when the music started, the kids didn't know whether to go left or right, so for a few moments there was mass confusion with everyone going in different directions until Mr. Christianson finally pointed to the right and we all started walking in the same direction.

Rivka and I didn't walk, we hopped. We hopped as best we could in the circle. She would hop once, then I would hop once. *Hop one, hop two. Repeat.* After a few times around, the costumed paraders started picking up speed. The faster the circle moved, the faster Rivka and I had to hop. Pretty soon some of the little kids were running in the circle and Rivka and I could scarcely keep up. We were both breathing heavy from all the hopping we were doing, all for the stupid prize of a blow-up elephant on a stick.

"Oh, forget it!" Rivka finally said. "I can't do this anymore." She suddenly stopped and didn't hop when she was supposed to, but I did, and

Rivka lost her footing because I was too far ahead of her, so the two of us tumbled in a conjoined heap to the floor. The parade circle of angels, princesses, cartoon characters, and assorted ghosts covered in motel-room sheets screeched to a halt so that everyone could laugh at us lying on the floor. And the sad part was, connected together the way we were, we couldn't get up. We struggled without success, but with her legs jammed into one pant leg, and my legs jammed into the other, we could not coordinate our two bodies to work as one. And how many people there offered to help us up? None! Not one single person! Because they were all too busy laughing at us flailing around on the floor in our unsuccessful attempt to stand up. All I have to say is if the Royal Rulers at school saw us at that moment, there would be no hope of being seen in the same universe as them again, no less being part of their clique.

Finally, Rivka cried out, "Daddy, help us!" and Mr. Christianson laughing as hard as the rest of the crowd grabbed one of Rivka's hands and one of mine, and pulled us up. So, you think after all that we would have at least won the Halloween costume contest, but nope...the blow-up elephant prize went to Reza Azar for being a robot made of aluminum foil.

After that, Rivka and I took our wounded prides back to her bedroom to separate our conjoined bodies. We spent the rest of the evening hiding from everyone and talking about how majorly lame the Halloween party was.

Chapter 15

By November, Rivka's and my social standings were improving at school. I was still doing math and science homework for Natalie and Cassandra, and in return, the Royal Rulers actually talked to me and Rivka. Fair trade, right? Although we weren't actually Royal Rulers, we definitely moved up a rung on the social ladder as the other kids at school started noticing the Royals were semi-friendly to us.

At home, Rivka held firm to her six-month prediction she made when we first arrived at the motel, and I started worrying she might be right. Thanksgiving was practically on top of us and there still was no sign of Mom getting a full-time job so we could afford to move out of the motel.

"What are we going to do about Thanksgiving dinner?" I asked my mother one day when she was sitting on her bed working on her laptop. "I don't think microwave turkey pot pies are going to cut it."

"I figured we'd go to a restaurant," Mom replied, not looking up.

"For Thanksgiving?"

"Lots of people eat out on Thanksgiving," Mom said. "It'll be nice, you'll see."

"It will be horrible," I grumbled.

I flopped down on my own bed and stared at the cracks in the ceiling.

"Mom?" I turned over on my side and watched my mother typing like a maniac on her keyboard.

"Hmmmm...."

"How much longer do you think we're going to live here?"

Mom stopped typing and looked over at me. Her eyes looked sad. "I don't know, Honey. I'm trying to save up enough money for a deposit on an apartment, but it's hard with the cost of food, and paying for this room, and insurance on the car, and... well...everything else."

"What about getting money from Dad? Does he even know where we are?"

"I called him. He knows."

"Doesn't he care that we're homeless?"

"We're not homeless, Cali," Mom said. "It's not like we're living in the car."

"But this isn't a real home, Mom! I can't invite my friends here. I can't tell anyone where we live. I can't even sleep in my own bed without Phoenix snoring in my ear every night."

Mom sighed. "You just have to be patient, Honey. Your dad and I have to work out the terms of our divorce. It's going to take time, so until everything gets sorted out, we might have to stay here awhile."

She turned back to her computer for a second then looked back at me. "Do you miss Dad?" she asked.

"Yeah, sometimes. But I don't miss the way you two used to fight."

"I don't miss that either."

"I miss our old house. And my old room."

"I know. I do too. But we need to make the best of living here for now. And...I need to get back to work so we get some money for a better life down the road." She turned her attention back to her laptop, and began clicking on the keys once again.

When I told Rivka how we were going to a restaurant for Thanksgiving, she mentioned it to her parents. I guess Mr. and Mrs. Christianson also figured spending Thanksgiving at a restaurant wasn't what the Pilgrims would have wanted because they came up with the idea of having a community dinner in the rec room. Everyone staying at the motel was invited. The week before Thanksgiving Rivka's parents had her go around to all the rooms to collect donations to help pay for food.

"How much is everyone contributing?" Mom asked when Rivka came to our room with an ice bucket she was using to hold the money.

"My parents were hoping each family would contribute $10 each," Rivka replied, "but they said whatever anyone can afford to give is fine."

Mom called the office to ask Mrs. Christianson if it was okay to give $5 now, and to give another $5 after she got some more cash in a day or two. After she hung up the phone, she said, "Rivka, your mother said don't forget to ask Malcolm if he wants to join us for Thanksgiving dinner."

"Thanksgiving with the creepy guy?" I cried.

"Cali, stop!" Mom scolded. "He's just a lonely old man."

I tagged along with Rivka as she continued collecting money from the other families, but when we spotted Old Man Malcolm sitting outside his room I hung back.

"I'll wait here while you go ask him for money," I said.

Rivka shook her head. "I'm not going over there alone."

"But if I stay here, I can run for help if he tries anything."

She grabbed my arm. "No way. You're coming with me." She pulled me towards Old Man Malcolm's room.

When we got close enough, Old Man Malcolm peered at us through his thick glasses.

Rivka stood a few feet away from him and I stood behind her. We were ready to dart towards the office if necessary.

"We're going to have Thanksgiving dinner in the rec room," Rivka said cautiously.

Old Man Malcolm didn't reply, he just squinted his eyes for a better look at us—probably trying to size up which one of us would be easier to grab and drag into his room.

"It will be this Thursday," Rivka continued.

Old Man Malcolm nodded his head, as if he made up his mind which of us would be easier prey.

"...For everyone in the motel," Rivka added.

Old Man Malcolm licked his lips.

"Would you like to come?" Rivka asked, her voice shaking a little.

"What time?" he asked.

"Dinner's at 1:00."

"Okay. I'll be there."

"Um...my parents are asking for contributions to help pay for the food."

"Oh...sure..." Old Man Malcolm took a wallet out of his pants pocket and pulled out a couple of twenty-dollar bills. He held them out to Rivka.

"That's too much," Rivka informed him. "We're only collecting $10 from each room."

"Take it, Missy," he replied. "Put it towards someone else's dinner in case they can't afford to pay."

The day before Thanksgiving, Mrs. Christianson, Mrs. Rivera, Mrs. Jones, and Mom went grocery shopping to buy enough food to feed an entire circus, while Rivka and I got stuck watching Pauly, Stacey, Georgia, the three Jones kids, and the three Rivera kids, all crammed into the Christiansons' apartment. Phoenix and Shannon were nowhere to be found to help us keep the kids from killing each other. When the shopping moms got home, they were joined by Mrs. Fitzpatrick and Mrs. Azar in the kitchen of the Christiansons' apartment, and we ended up with two more kids in our care—Isabella and Reza. The mothers set about cooking three turkeys, tons of mashed potatoes, stuffing, vegetables, sweet potatoes, pies, and enough food to feed the entire motel population. They cooked all day, and by evening every miniature-sized refrigerator in every efficiency room in the motel was filled to capacity with food. The next day, each family had to heat up stuff in the microwave oven of their room, or on hot plates if they had them. By noon every kid in the motel old enough to understand directions was put to work arranging the tables and chairs in the rec room.

Then everyone helped cart food from the rooms or the Christiansons' kitchen to the rec hall. Everything went without mishap until Roberto dropped an entire pumpkin pie on the floor, and blamed it on Hector, who blamed it on Pauly, who blamed it on Roberto. When the entire motel population sat down to their reheated-in-a-microwave Thanksgiving meal, Mrs. Christianson, said in a loud voice, "This feels like Christmas in Whoville."

All the adults laughed and agreed with her. Rivka looked at me and rolled her eyes in embarrassment at her mother's lame comment.

"Should we all hold hands and sing?" Mom asked.

Again, the adults laughed, and this time, I was the one rolling my eyes.

As we ate the Thanksgiving meal, it was hard to hear anything anyone said, since everyone was talking at the same time. Phoenix and Shannon were sitting a few seats down from where Rivka and I were. I don't think I've ever seen Phoenix looking as happy as she did during dinner because she had managed to snag a seat next to Michael Fitzpatrick. She barely touched her food, because she was too busy leaning over to MicFitz and yapping in his ear. I never saw him say anything back.

After dinner the adults and older kids, which unfortunately included Rivka and me, cleaned off the tables and put away the left-over food, while the little kids ran wild around the rec room. It didn't take long for Roberto, Hector, and Pauly to start chasing and terrorizing the younger kids, and Mr. Christianson had to yell at them a few times to cut it out. After Old Man Malcolm shook his cane at the boys, that's when they finally piped down. I guess none of them wanted to be Malcolm's next victim.

    Once the tables were all cleaned off, Mr. Fitzpatrick left the rec room and came back with a guitar. He encouraged everyone to gather around him as he strummed a few medleys. When he started singing "The Wheels on the Bus," everyone from two-year-old Benjamin up to Old Man Malcolm joined in the singing. Even Mr. Azar who never talks was singing along, although it seemed like he was singing different words than the rest of us. I mostly lipped synced so as not to be embarrassed by my frog-toned singing voice. After several more sing-along songs, Shannon, showoff that she was, got up and sang a solo while accompanied by Mr. Fitzpatrick's guitar playing. She kept sneaking peeks at Michael while she sang, but he was sitting in a corner with his nose in a book and didn't appear to be paying any attention to her.

    After an hour of musical entertainment, Jodi's kids started getting all whiny and tired, Pauly was bugging the bones out of everyone, and the Rivera boys were getting antsy to destroy something, so everyone started heading back to their rooms. All things considered, it turned out to be a pretty decent Thanksgiving.

Chapter 16

December 1st was the six-month anniversary of my family living in the motel. I tried not to acknowledge it at all, but sure enough, Rivka came out of her apartment that morning doing the victory dance.

"I knew it! I knew it!" she sang, jumping around the parking lot.

"Oh, shut up," I grumbled.

"From the day you arrived, I knew you'd be here six months. So once again, my prediction was correct!"

"Not true! Unless we move out today, we'll be here for *more* than six months so your prediction is wrong."

"I said you'd be here at LEAST six months."

"No, you said I'd be here FOR six months."

"Give it up, Cali. I am psychic and you refuse to believe it."

"You refuse to believe that you are NOT psychic."

Even if the so-called psychic predicted I'd be living in this place for six months, I never imagined I'd be living here that long. Spending Thanksgiving at the motel was one thing, but being here come Christmas was something I couldn't even begin to imagine. As the days inched towards Christmas, the idea of celebrating it in the motel grew more depressing. I suppose I wasn't the only one who thought that either. Most of the people living at Langster seemed a little down as the month went on.

It wasn't until the week before Christmas, that the mood changed. One day, Mr. Christianson and Mr. Fitzpatrick went out together in the Langstermobile and came home with a giant tree tied to the roof of the van. As they drove into the parking lot, Mr. Christianson laid on the Langstermobile's horn until everyone came out of their rooms to see what the commotion was about.

"TREE TRIMMING IN THE REC ROOM!" Mr. Christianson shouted.

He and Mr. Fitzpatrick started untying the tree from the top of the van, and then Michael, Mr. Azar, and a bunch of other parents rushed over to help them. It took eight people to pull the tree off the roof of the Langstermobile and carry it to the rec room, while about twenty-five little kids followed them, squealing like excited little piglets.

"OUTTA THE WAY!" Mr. Christianson kept yelling as kids danced around them. Mrs. Fitzpatrick steered the kids over to a table where Mrs. Christianson, Mrs. Jones, and Mom had dumped boxes of decorations and assorted craft supplies. To keep them from bugging the fathers setting up the tree, the mothers got the younger kids involved in making pipe cleaner and bead decorations. There were fits of giggles from the younger kids every time Rivka's father let out a string of swears as he and the other men struggled to get the trunk of the tree into the stand.

"LANGUAGE!" his wife kept yelling over to him.

As soon as the tree was up, the parents let the kids loose to decorate it with the hand-made ornaments and all the cheesy plastic objects that had been purchased at a dollar store. The kids loaded all the ornaments on the bottom of the tree. Since none of them could reach very high, the adults got involved moving ornaments towards the top. Rivka predicted the tree would look like crap when it was done, but in the end, it actually didn't look half-bad.

After the tree was decorated, Michael Fitzpatrick came in the rec room carrying a box. It was filled with hand-knitted stockings that Mrs. Fitzpatrick had made for every kid at the motel.

"Wowie, you make all these?" Mrs. Azar asked, holding one up.

Mrs. Fitzpatrick just smiled and nodded.

"*Yew* sure outdid *yew-self*, Sugar," Mrs. Jones said, picking up a stocking and examining it. "These are simply scrumptious!"

All the other mothers joined in, making a huge fuss over the knitted stockings. It was easy to see that the barebones rec room was short on fireplaces, so the kids ended up hanging their stockings on the walls with thumbtacks. It was like a Christmas miracle in itself that Mr. Christianson didn't yell about all the pin holes we were putting in the walls.

Everyone was getting along pretty well during the tree-trimming party up until Pauly, Roberto, and Hector started chasing Gabby, Isabella, and the Jones girls around the room. The girls started screaming in terror, then Mrs. Rivera and Mr. Christenson started yelling at the boys to stop, and before you knew it, the entire room erupted in craziness. That's when Rivka and I left, in case any of the parents got the idea to have us watch their kids while they sat around drinking a secret stash of spiked eggnog.

At seven-thirty Christmas morning, Mom, Georgia, Phoenix and I arrived at the rec room and it looked like we were one of the last ones there. Many of the kids were already rifling through their stockings, while others were running around the room in excitement. Not long after we arrived, Santa came in the room looking remarkably like Mr. Christianson, and bellowing loudly like him too. Santa passed out the presents to all the kids, even the older kids like me and Phoenix. I have no idea who paid for the gifts, but I suspect all the parents bought their own child something and stuck it in Santa's sack. I got a makeup bag filled with eyeliner, mascara, blush, lipstick, and some nail polish—all of which I really, really wanted. Whether it was Santa or Mom, someone obviously knew I needed my own makeup because Phoenix was getting tired of me using up all hers.

"Come on, everyone! Breakfast!" Mrs. Christianson yelled. The mothers had set out a spread of donuts, muffins, pastries, fruit, yogurt, and juice. Mostly the adults ate because the kids were too busy playing with their new toys.

In the afternoon, the moms brought in more food, and the entire day was spent eating and playing. Mr. Christianson hooked up the karaoke machine, and a bunch of kids made fools of themselves singing songs with it, and a bunch of the adults made even bigger fools of themselves by getting up and singing too. Rivka got up and did a song with Georgia and Stacey, but no amount of begging or threatening from Rivka could get me up there with them.

Karaoke reached an all-time embarrassing high when Mrs. Azar, Mrs. Jones, and Mrs. Rivera got up and sang some oldie song about bad girls. The audience was screeching with laughter at how bad their singing was, not to mention Mrs. Azar's bad pronunciation of the words. Suddenly there was a huge crash and everyone in the room jumped, kids screamed, the Hudson baby started crying, and the Karaoke Bad Girls never got to finish their song.

"ROBERTO!" Mrs. Rivera screamed into the microphone she was holding in her hand.

"I DIDN'T DO IT, MA!" Roberto yelled, as he, Hector, Pauly, and Reza all ran from the toppled Christmas tree covering a massive portion of the rec room. Ornaments littered the floor all around it, and some ornaments even rolled to the other side of the room. Mr. Christianson, Mr. Fitzpatrick, Mr. Azar, and a bunch of the mothers surrounded the fallen tree, while the tree-toppling boys cowered on the opposite side of the room with guilt smeared all over their faces.

"Let's get this thing back up," Mr. Christianson ordered. Rivka and I joined the group of parents and the high school kids to set the ten-foot-tall tree back up. It took longer to put up the second time than the first, probably because Mr. Christianson insisted the tree be tied and anchored with twenty feet of rope to be sure even a record-breaking earthquake wouldn't bring it down again.

Everyone old enough to walk helped pick up the ornaments that were strewn all over the room and for the second time we decorated the tree. The only ones who didn't pitch in were Roberto, Hector, Pauly, and Reza. The guilty quartet stayed as far away from the tree as possible, knowing they were totally in for it once their parents got them back in their rooms. If I were any of them, I would pack my bags right now and go join the Army.

Not long after the tree came down, the tree topplers were arm-escorted out by their parents. Everyone else packed up their gifts and headed back to their rooms.

Chapter 17

When we returned to school after Christmas vacation, I got sucked right back into doing Natalie's and Cassandra's homework in addition to my own.

"When are you going to stop doing it for them?" Rivka asked. "It's not right."

"Soon," I promised.

"You've been saying that since the first week you started."

"I'm trying to figure out a good way of telling them I can't, without them getting mad at me."

I wouldn't admit to Rivka that doing their homework didn't feel right to me either, but after a few more weeks, my homework brown-nosing paid off for us again. It happened one day before math class. As I handed Cassandra a copy of the homework problems, Phoebe looked over and said, "California Girl, you should sit with us at lunch."

If I hadn't already been sitting down, I probably would have fallen on the floor. Trying to act as if an invite to sit with the Royal Rulers wasn't that big a deal, I asked, "Today?"

"Today's cool," Phoebe replied.

"And Rivka too?"

"Sure," Phoebe replied before the teacher came in the room and told everyone to quiet down.

Instead of paying attention for the rest of class I worried myself into a frenzy thinking maybe this was a trick. Maybe as soon as Rivka and I got to their table, the Royal Rulers would tell us there wasn't room again. Yet, at lunch, when we went to their table Natalie looked as if she was about to tell us to get lost, but before she could say anything, Phoebe said to Rivka, "Your taco looks gross," which I think translated to, "Welcome to our table."

"We're practically one of them, Rivka," I said that afternoon as we hung out in Rivka's living room.

"Really? Because I still feel like an outsider with them. I'm actually more comfortable around Bernice and Monica."

"Yeah, but Bernice and Monica are nerdy kids. Which means, by association, we are too if we hang out with them."

"But they're real. The Royals are all-fake like."

"If you want to be popular, Rivka, you have to hang out with the popular people."

"Maybe so, but Hailey's neediness is tons more irritating than Bernice's sneezing."

It was true. Whenever Hailey said anything, she'd look at Phoebe for approval, and if Phoebe ignored her, which she did all the time, she'd look to Natalie for some kind of response. When Natalie ignored her, she'd latch on to Cassandra. She really was needy, but I couldn't talk because in a way, I was needy too. I needed them all if I was ever going to be popular.

The next day at lunch, I walked over to the Royals table with Rivka following.

"Do you have room for two more?" I asked, hoping we wouldn't be humiliated again by being told there was no room.

Whether it was in payment for my diligent homework efforts or because Phoebe just wanted to annoy Natalie by letting us sit with them again, Phoebe nodded and said, "Sure. Sit."

From then on, Rivka and I were permitted to sit with the Royals at lunch each day. Every day that we sat at their table I felt less like the nerdy girl I used to be, and more like someone special. Even though after school I was still just a simple motel dweller with no control over my life, at school I was finally becoming a Royal.

Chapter 18

When the weather started warming up some, child-crazed parents shooed their kids out of their motel rooms. Naturally, that meant Rivka and I were once again the most sought-after babysitters in all the land--or at least at the motel. One March day, Rivka and I were sitting under a budding tree watching Jodi's four kids, when Mrs. Jones came out of her room and over to us, with her two daughters following close behind.

"It *shore* would be nice for my lil pumpkins to get some fresh air," she said. "Y'all don't mind watchin' 'em while I do some cleaning in our room, do *yew*?"

Rivka and I exchanged dismayed looks. Mrs. Jones took that to mean yes.

"I'm *shore* they won't be any trouble," she said, nudging her girls off towards the sandbox. She headed back to her room without a second glance.

No sooner had she gone, when Jodi's baby started fussing in the baby carrier.

Rivka looked at her nervously. "Quick, Cali, do something, before she starts screaming again."

I picked up Juliana and started bouncing her gently in my arms.

A few moments later, Mrs. Rivera came out of her room, followed by Hector and Roberto.

"Cali! Rivka!" she called over to us. "I need you to keep an eye on these boys for me, will you?"

"Was that a question?" I whispered to Rivka.

"Hardly," she whispered back.

"You two stay where the girls can see you," Mrs. Rivera said, pushing her sons towards us.

Without waiting for us to tell her we absolutely did not want to watch her evil offspring, Mrs. Rivera got in her car and drove off with Gabby, the only child she gave birth to that didn't terrorize every living being around her.

"See ya later!" Roberto said, as he ran towards the back of the motel.

"Later," Hector said taking off after him.

"Don't look at me," I said hugging Jodi's baby protectively. "I'm not going after them."

"Let 'em stay back there," Rivka said, "At least they're not bugging us."

When Mrs. Rivera returned a couple of hours later with Gabby, she came clacking across the parking lot to the sandbox where we were breaking up a sand fight. Mrs. Rivera's frosted hair was puffed up, adding an inch to her small height. It also looked greener than usual. Gabby had her long black hair pulled back in a French braid. Obviously, the two Rivera females had been to a hair salon together.

"Where's Hector and Roberto?" Mrs. Rivera asked.

"I think they're around back in the clubhouse," I replied, restraining one of the Hudson boys from throwing a shovel at his twin brother.

"Why aren't you keeping an eye on them?" she cried. "You know what kind of trouble they get into when they're not watched!"

"But we're watching all these kids and the boys ran off," I explained.

"We can't leave the little ones to go chase after them," Rivka added, struggling with the other Hudson twin.

"Well, if you girls can't keep an eye on them like you're supposed to, don't come asking me for a reference when you want to get a real babysitting job."

I opened my eyes wide and looked at Rivka. *Did we ever say we wanted a reference? Or even a babysitting job?*

Mrs. Rivera stormed off to the back of the motel to find Hector and Roberto, leaving Gabby in our care.

The next day, Rivka and I switched our hiding place from the back steps of the motel to the back seat of the Langstermobile. Whenever someone walked by the van, we ducked down, hoping they wouldn't see us. When parents discovered that hiding place, we switched to hiding in the bathroom of my room again, but every time we were in there, Georgia or one of her friends would bang on the door trying to get in to use it.

One night, I was lying in bed thinking about other possible places Rivka and I could hide, when I saw through the window curtains the headlights of a car in the parking lot. The clock on the bedside table said it was three o'clock. For the record that was 3:00 *a.m.* The reason I was awake at that time was because Mom's and

Phoenix's snoring had woken me up--*again*. So, in addition to lying there trying to think of new places Rivka and I could hide to avoid babysitting, I was lying there wishing I had a pair of earplugs. Over the snoring, I heard a couple of car doors open and shut, and then the sound of a motel room door shutting before everything outside went quiet. I only wished everything in our own room was as quiet.

At nine-thirty the next morning there was a knock on our door. It was Saturday, so everyone was still in the room. When Mom answered the door, Mrs. Christianson was standing there. She motioned for my mother to come outside and she and Mom talked in low voices in the parking lot. They were soon joined by Mrs. Fitzpatrick, Mrs. Rivera, and Mrs. Jones.

Rivka was already outside, and when she saw our door open, she came over to our room.

"What are all the moms gossiping about?" I asked.

"The new family that checked in early this morning," Rivka said.

"There's a new family here?" Georgia asked, coming up behind us.

Rivka nodded.

"Any kids our age?" I asked.

Rivka gave me her "get-real" look. "No such luck. A seven-year-old boy and nine-year-old girl."

"Yippee!!!" Georgia cried, running out of the room.

"Darnit!" I kicked the door jamb. "Two more kids to babysit."

"Let's go eavesdrop," Rivka said.

Limping from the pain after my kick, we joined the group that was growing larger by the minute in the parking lot.

"They're probably going to be staying here at least a month, maybe longer," Mrs. Christianson was saying.

"I predict five months," Rivka whispered to me.

Ignoring her I strained to hear the mothers better.

"Oh, those poor lil' dumplin's," said Mrs. Jones.

"They *lose* everything?" Mrs. Azar asked.

"They arrived wearing only their pajamas. Other than their car, pretty much everything else they owned was lost in the fire."

"Did their house blow up?" Roberto asked excitedly. His mother told him to shut up.

Soon, almost everyone from the motel had joined the group in the parking lot to talk about the new arrivals. Mr. and Mrs. Sullivan and their children, Anita and Dwight, had come to Langster Motel because their house over on Hedgewood Street had caught fire and burned to the ground.

"They're going to need help getting back on their feet," Mrs. Christianson said to the group.

"What can we do to help?" Mrs. Fitzpatrick asked.

"Maybe we can collect some things they need," I said. Everyone looked over at me. "You know, clothing and stuff."

"That's a great idea, Cali," Mrs. Christianson said.

"Maybe some of Hakeem's clothes might fit the boy," Mrs. Jones offered.

"Georgia has some clothes that might fit the girl," Mom said.

"Anyone know about what size the father is?" Mr. Fitzpatrick asked. "I could give him some clothes I have if they'll fit him."

"I have plenty of clothes I don't wear that the mother could have as well," Mrs. Fitzpatrick added.

"Maybe *skool* supplies?" Mrs. Azar suggested. "We have extras."

"They'll probably need food too," Mrs. Rivera said.

After tossing around a bunch of suggestions, everyone went back to their rooms to see what they could donate to the fire victims. Boxes and bags began piling up outside the office. With a couple of ice buckets as collection baskets, Rivka and I went knocking on every door at the motel to see if we could collect some money for the Sullivan family fund. It was almost like being on a scavenger hunt for money. Even though the people at the motel couldn't afford to give much, almost everyone gave a little. Rivka and I argued over which one of us would ask Old Man Malcolm if he wanted to donate anything.

"I asked him at Thanksgiving," Rivka said. "It's your turn."

"But, you're braver than I am."

"Oh please...you're way braver than me."

"Fine! I'll do it!" I grabbed the ice bucket from her. "But if I end up with the words 'Simmons Beauty Rest' imprinted on my face, you're the one that has to live with the guilt."

I marched over to Old Man Malcolm, while Rivka stood a safe distance away. After I told him the story of the Sullivans, he slowly got out of his chair and motioned me to follow him inside his room. I looked over at Rivka and she shook her head warning me not to go. Determined not to show how scared I was, I took a few cautious steps inside his room, leaving the door wide open for quick escape. A few moments later, I came back out and went over to a Rivka.

"Cali! Are you okay?" she whispered seeing how stunned I must have looked. "What did he do to you?"

"You are not going to believe it," I said in a low voice so only she could hear.

Rivka's eyes grew bigger. "What did you see in there?" she asked. "Any dead bodies?"

I shook my head, then held up the $100 bill Old Man Malcolm had placed in the ice bucket. Rivka looked as if she might faint.

After we finished taking up our collection and delivered it to Rivka's parents, Mom, Mrs. Rivera, Jodi, and Mrs. Fitzpatrick drove off in the Fitzpatricks' car to go to Spendmart. Mr. Christianson, Mr. Azar, and Mr. Fitzpatrick climbed into the Langstermobile for a trip to The Home Depot. Mrs. Christianson, Mrs. Jones, and Mrs. Azar headed to the Christiansons' kitchen to do some cooking. Shannon, Phoenix, Michael, Rivka, and I all had the task of watching the younger kids so their parents could shop, cook, or run errands. For the first time, Rivka and I didn't complain about watching the kids for free.

"Why don't we try to raise more money for the Sullivans?" Phoenix said to the group of kids hanging around in the side yard.

"We could have a bake sale," Shannon offered.

"We don't bake," Rivka reminded her.

"How about a lemonade stand instead?" I suggested.

"That's a good idea," Phoenix said. "We could set up a table at the end of the parking lot and sell lemonade."

"And maybe we could sell some candy too," I added.

"Yeah! Candy! Candy! Candy!" a bunch of kids started jumping up and down.

"Where are we going to get candy to sell?" Georgia asked.

"Mom has a whole bag of candy bars stashed in our room," I said.

"Yeah, we have some candy in our room too," Hakeem offered.

"My mom won't let us have sugar because it makes us too wild," Roberto griped.

"Do you have any snack bars or Fruit Snacks?" Shannon asked.

"Yeah, we have some snack bars," Roberto said.

"We have Fruit Snacks in our room," Andrew and Brian said in unison.

Shannon turned to Michael Fitzpatrick. "Michael, would you mind getting a table from the rec room and bringing it up near the road?"

Michael nodded, and Phoenix quickly offered to help him.

"The rest of you kids go to your rooms and see if you can find any good snacks we can sell," Shannon instructed. "We only want things that are individually wrapped. Don't bring back anything stupid like a giant bag of potato chips, understand?"

All the kids ran to their rooms to forage for goodies.

"Come on, Rivka and Cali," Shannon said, "Let's go make lemonade and some signs."

The three of us headed off to the Christiansons' apartment while Michael and Phoenix went to the rec room to get a table. By the time we came back outside with three large containers of lemonade and a half a dozen signs, a table had already been set up at the edge of the parking lot, and was piled up with an assortment of snacks the kids had found in their rooms. The younger kids took turns holding up the signs by the side of the road and they all waved and tried to get drivers to stop by yelling, "Lemonade! Candy!"

We discovered that Roberto had a hidden talent that might possibly lead to a future as a salesman. More so than anyone else, he managed to get cars to stop by screaming at them until he was blue in the face, and once they stopped, he bullied them into buying more stuff than they wanted. By the time we ran out of lemonade and snacks, we had raised another $43.25 for the Sullivan family.

Several hours later, everyone assembled in the parking lot again, this time in front of the Sullivans' room. After Mrs. Christianson knocked on the door of Room 3, a man dressed in a tee-shirt and lounge pants opened the door. He looked surprised to see so many people standing there. His wife came up behind him, then their son and daughter, all wearing pajamas. The

Sullivans stared at the group of strangers holding bags of groceries, plates of food, armloads of clothing, toys, and assorted household items.

"Mr. and Mrs. Sullivan," Rivka's mother began, "I hope you don't mind, but I told the other residents of the motel about your house fire. Everyone here wanted to help, so we gathered up a few things that we thought you could use. They're yours if you want them."

One by one, people went up to the Sullivan family and placed something in their arms or at their feet; a bag of clothing, some toys, a casserole, a cake, some groceries, gift cards to stores, the leftover cash from everyone's donations, as well as the money from the lemonade and snack sale.

Mr. Sullivan stood there just shaking his head. Mrs. Sullivan started to thank everyone, but before she finished, she burst into tears. All the moms hurried over to her and one by one gave her a hug and told her if they needed anything to just ask. Many of the moms had tears rolling down their cheeks, and when the little kids saw their moms crying, they starting crying too. I have to admit, my eyes were filling up, but I managed to rub them and stop the tears from escaping before anyone thought I was a total wuss or something, but when I looked over at Phoenix and Shannon, I saw they were both fighting back the waterworks too. Even Old Man Malcolm's crusty old eyes looked watery.

That day, another family came to live at the Langster Motel, destined to stay indefinitely. Unlike when my family first arrived at Langster, this family didn't just move into a motel. They joined a community.

Chapter 19

By the time spring arrived, I felt like we'd never move out of the motel. Mom was still trying to find full-time work, but nothing she applied for came through. So far, Rivka and I managed to keep anyone at school from finding out that we lived at the motel. We were now sitting with the Royal Rulers every day at lunch and sometimes going places with them on the weekends, and even they didn't suspect that we were motel dwellers. As far as they knew, I lived in a normal house where I sat around all day doing their homework for them. And yes, I knew the homework thing was why they even allowed us in their clique, but I considered it an admission fee that had to be paid to get in. Rivka and I were becoming well known at Lincoln Middle School because, by process of association, we were practically Royal Rulers too.

One day our English teacher announced that we were going to have to write and give a speech in front of the class. Our speeches had to start out with "I bet you didn't know..." and we were to tell something about ourselves that most of our classmates don't know. It could be about a talent we have, a place we've lived, or an accomplishment of ours. It was bad enough worrying about what I was going to give my speech about, but I was dreading the thought that one of the Royals would ask me to write their speech for them. I didn't know how I was going to say no to that, but even I had my limits.

As I figured it would, the subject of our English speech came up at the Royal Rulers' table a few days later during lunch, and I sat there with pins jabbing my stomach, fully expecting to have the task of writing a speech or two for someone else dumped on me.

"Anyone know yet what they're going to talk about?" asked Hailey, darting a glance with her tiny black eyes, first to Natalie, then to Phoebe who was too busy texting under the table to notice.

"I know what I'm talking about!" Cassandra bragged.

"Let me guess," Natalie said. "You're going to talk about being an actress."

Cassandra looked surprised, as if she hadn't bragged constantly about all the plays she's been in. "How'd you know?" she asked.

Natalie shrugged. "Lucky guess."

"What about you?" Cassandra asked Natalie. "What are you going to talk about?"

The pins jabbed deeper in my stomach and I nervously picked at my lower lip as I waited for the inevitable: Natalie asking me what I was going to write up for her.

"I haven't decided on a topic yet," Natalie said. "Cali, do you have any ideas?"

"Ideas about what I'm giving my speech on?"

"No, about what I should give *my* speech on."

I didn't even know what I was going to do my own speech on, no less hers too. I shook my head.

"Maybe I'll talk about boys," she said. "Maybe my speech will be, 'I bet you didn't know I could get any boy I want'."

Phoebe, who had been quiet up to that point, looked up at me and just rolled her eyes.

Natalie saw it. "I suppose you're going to talk about your famous mother."

"Why would you suppose that?" Phoebe asked.

"You know everyone wants to hear about her," Natalie replied. "I bet anything you'd get an automatic A."

Phoebe pulled the cell phone she had been hiding from the lunch monitors out from under the table. "My mother is the last thing I'd talk about," she said, tucking her phone into a pocket of her leather jacket.

Deciding her lunch was over even though the bell hadn't rung yet, Phoebe got up and walked out of the cafeteria without any of the lunch monitors trying to stop her. You had to admire the power she had over the school staff.

After she left, the conversation went from our English speech to the rumors circulating around the school about how Sara Spindle was caught making out with Kevin Moyer behind the school yesterday. By the time lunch ended, the nervous fluttering in my stomach eased a little and I was thankful I didn't have to tell Natalie or anyone else I wouldn't do their speech for them. At least for now, anyway.

As Rivka and I walked to the bus together after school I asked her about her own speech. "Have you decided yet what you're going to talk about?"

"I don't know. Do you think I should talk about being psychic?"

"Whoa! No...not a good idea," I warned her.

"It might be interesting to everyone," Rivka said.

"It will probably get you condemned to the Social Funny Farm."

"You really think so?"

"Absolutely. What's your Plan B speech?" I asked.

"I don't have one," Rivka said.

"Well, you're ahead of me. I don't even have a Plan A speech yet," I admitted.

We got on the bus and headed for a seat in the back. As the bus filled with students, the noise level continued to rise. When the bus was full, the bus driver stood up.

"Listen up everyone!" she shouted over the noise. When everyone had quieted down, she announced, "There's been a slight change in the bus route so some of you will be let off a little later than you're used to, and some of you will be getting home a little earlier."

There were some cheers and a few moans from the kids.

"Hey, bus driver!" Aaron Depasko shouted from his seat. "Drop me off first!"

One of his friends shouted, "Dude, someone already dropped you—ON YOUR HEAD."

Aaron shouted again, "On second thought, drop this kid off first before I throw him out the window."

The two boys pretended to wrestle with each other while all their friends laughed. As the bus driver pulled the bus out of the school parking lot, she shouted over her shoulder, "Sit down you two before I make you both get off right now."

The first stop was the corner of Hamilton Avenue and the handful of kids whose stop it was let out whoops and cheers as they got off the bus earlier than they had anticipated. After Hamilton Avenue, Rivka and I were horrified when the bus stopped in front of the motel.

"What are we going to do?" Rivka asked in a panicked voice.

"Quick, duck down!" I whispered.

We crouched in our seats, hoping the driver didn't see us. The driver scanned the bus from the rearview mirror. "Anyone getting off here?" she yelled from her seat. When no one replied, she closed the door and drove on.

"Now what?" Rivka whispered.

"We'll get off at the next stop and walk back," I said in a low voice.

The next stop ended up being over near Meadow Street.

When we got off, the driver said, "Hey, don't you two get off at the motel?"

"Nope," we both said at the same time and hurried off the bus.

Aaron Depasko also got off on Meadow Street, but Rivka and I hurried away before he questioned why we were getting off at his stop. The walk back to the motel was longer than we expected. When we finally got to the motel, we dropped our backpacks on the ground in the side yard, and plopped down next to them.

"So, what happens tomorrow morning if there are already kids on the bus when it stops here?" Rivka said, wiping the sweat off her forehead with her sleeve.

"I'm not sure." I pondered it for a moment. "I think we need to change our morning bus stop too."

"You want to walk to Meadow Street every morning before school?" Rivka looked ready to barf.

"What choice do we have? We can't take a chance someone might see us picked up here."

"We can tell them that story about our houses being behind the woods and for some stupid reason they made this motel the bus stop."

"I don't know if they'll buy it. Especially now that we know there are no houses back there."

"There are plenty of houses two blocks down on the other side of Route 9. We'll tell them we live over there."

"They wouldn't have kids cross Route 9 to catch the bus on this side."

"What about Aaron? What are we going to tell him when he starts seeing us at his stop every day?"

"We'll just tell him our old stop got eliminated."

"You think he'll believe that?"

"Would you rather he sees us picked up in front of the motel?"

"Cali, can't we just tell everyone we live two blocks away from here?"

I gave her one of my mother's quit-arguing-with-me looks. "I'm waking you up early tomorrow and we're walking to Meadow Street."

The next morning half asleep, Rivka and I headed out for the quarter-mile walk to our new bus stop. As soon as Aaron spotted us, he came over. "What are you two doing here?" he asked.

"They eliminated our stop in the change," I lied. "So now we get picked up and dropped off here."

Aaron just shrugged. "Oh," was all he said, before he headed over to a group of boys where he started joking around with them. Maybe boys don't read into things as much as girls do.

After the bus picked us up, the next stop was the motel. I crouched down in my seat as we got closer, and pushed Rivka down too, just in case anyone from the motel was outside when we passed and spotted us. The bus slowed down, but not seeing anyone waiting at the end of the parking lot, the driver drove on.

"Goodbye motel bus stop. Hello Meadow Street," I whispered.

"I've got a bad feeling about this," Rivka muttered.

Chapter 20

The next morning, I went to meet Rivka outside her apartment before we headed off to our new bus stop.

"Where are you two going so early?" Mr. Christianson asked, coming out of the laundry room with a pile of clean sheets in his arms.

"To catch the bus," Rivka answered.

Mr. Christianson glanced at his watch. "This early?"

"We're walking over to Meadow Street to catch the bus there," Rivka said.

"What's wrong with waiting for it in front of the motel?"

"It doesn't stop here anymore," Rivka lied.

"What? It's supposed to!"

"They changed the route so now we get picked up at the Meadow Street stop."

"You've got to be kidding!" Mr. Christianson exclaimed. "What are they thinking making you two walk that far?"

"It's not that far, Dad."

"It must be at least a mile to Meadow Street."

"It's not a mile, Dad, and we like walking!"

"Well, no kid of mine is walking that far to catch a bus. I'm calling the bus company right now!"

"Dad! No!"

"Don't you girls worry...one phone call and I'll have this whole thing straightened out with the bus company." Mr. Christianson went inside to make the call.

Rivka looked at me in desperation. "I told you I had a bad feeling about this, Cali."

"Well, why did you tell him where we were going?"

"Because he asked!"

Inside the office we heard Mr. Christianson yelling at some poor bus company employee. I grabbed Rivka's hand. "Come on, let's get out of here before he finds out they didn't really eliminate the stop."

The next morning when I went to meet Rivka to head out to Meadow Street, Mr. Christianson followed her out of the office.

"Good news, Cali," he said. "You two don't have to walk to the next stop. The bus is going to stop right in front of the motel to pick you up." He then headed off in the direction of the rec room.

"Thank you, Dad," Rivka said, sarcastically.

When he was out of sight, I grabbed Rivka's arm. "Come on, let's go!"

"Go where?"

"To Meadow Street! Before your dad sees us!"

"I can't go to Meadow Street now after my dad spent an hour on the phone yelling at the bus company about not stopping here anymore."

"We can't let the kids see us picked up here."

"We have no choice, Cali."

"Maybe you don't, but I do."

"What do you mean?"

"If you're not coming with me to Meadow Street, then I'll go alone."

"What? You're not going to wait here with me?"

"With or without you, I'm still going to Meadow Street. I'm not letting everyone on the bus see me picked up in front of the motel."

"So, you're throwing me to the wolves while you save yourself."

"What good will it do if we both get eaten by wolves?"

Rivka looked hurt. "A fine friend you are," she grumbled.

I walked to Meadow Street alone, feeling like I had pushed my best friend under the wheels of the school bus while I stood on the curb and watched. But what could I do? No sense in both of us going down, right? I sat alone until the next stop when the bus picked Rivka up at the end of the motel parking lot, the Langster Motel sign jeering at me through the bus window. Rivka hurried down the bus aisle and slipped into the seat beside me. "Is anyone staring?" she whispered.

I looked around. "Nope. I don't think anyone even noticed the motel."

"Great. Then this afternoon you'll get off at the motel with me?"

I shook my head. "No, thank you."

"Chicken!"

And so that's how it came to be that Rivka and I who lived less than a hundred feet away from each other now had two different bus stops; she because her big-mouthed father wanted his daughter to have all the conveniences she was entitled to, and me because I was a total chicken.

Chapter 21

Rivka didn't give up trying to make me feel guilty about it, but I managed to build up a small level of immunity from the guilt of not waiting with her every morning at the motel bus stop. One morning after the bus picked her up and she slid into the seat next to me, she griped, "I really don't see the benefit of you going all the way to Meadow Street every morning by yourself when you could just walk to the end of the parking lot to get picked up."

"One benefit is that I'm toning up in the right places with all this walking," I informed her.

"...Not to mention you get to sleep later in the morning if you get picked up at the motel," she said, acting as if she hadn't heard me.

"I only have to leave a half hour earlier. It's not a big deal since I'm usually awake that early anyway because of the snore fest going on in my room."

"I don't know how you can live with yourself knowing I'm standing at the motel stop alone every morning. You're supposed to be supportive and stay with me."

"I'm being supportive by staying on the bus to defend you if anyone says anything."

"Why, what are they saying?" she asked, looking horrified.

"Nothing, I said *if* anyone says anything, I'm there to watch your back."

"But no one's said anything?"

"Nope." I tried to sound convincing.

"Good, then they won't say anything if you get picked up there either."

At school we went to our lockers and headed to homeroom together. "By the way, I won't be taking the bus home this afternoon," Rivka said.

"Did you decide to walk home so you aren't seen getting off at the motel anymore?" I joked.

"Real funny, Cali." She whacked my arm lightly with her science book. "My mom is picking me up for a dentist appointment. Maybe by the time I'm done getting all my teeth cleaned, you'll finally be home from your long-distance bus stop walk."

"Oooh…impressive comeback," I said, returning the smack with my own science book.

That afternoon, instead of waiting to walk to the bus with Rivka as I usually did, I followed the Royal Rulers out of the school, like a puppy on the heels of my masters.

"What is that?" Natalie asked, stopping suddenly and causing me to crash into her, *yet again*, only this time she was too interested in something else to care.

My eyes followed where Natalie was staring. Sitting in the pickup car line was the Langstermobile, complete with the sign lit up on the top. It stood out like a bloody wound in the lineup of Hondas, Toyotas, and soccer mom vans. Mr. Christianson was behind the wheel.

"I think it's some kind of hearse," Cassandra said.

"Ohhhhh...do you think there's a dead body in there?" Hailey asked.

"I don't think they'd have the sign lit up on top if they had a dead body in there," Natalie said.

"You morons," Phoebe said. "Hearses don't have light-up signs on top."

I swear, within 40 seconds, it was like every kid coming out of the school stopped and stared at the Langstermobile, some of them laughing, some pointing at it, others looking confused as they tried to figure out what planet this mothership came from. I mean...it's like they never saw a Langstermobile before!

I stood behind Phoebe and Natalie and kept my head down in case Mr. Christianson spotted me and waved or something.

Rivka came up behind me, using both me and the other two girls as a shield.

"*What's he doing here?*" I whispered to her as she hid behind me.

"*I don't know. My mom was supposed to pick me up,*" she whispered back.

Natalie was still staring at the van. "That is the most hideous vehicle I've ever seen," she said in a loud voice, making sure everyone standing in front of the school heard.

"*Please, just kill me now,*" Rivka whispered.

"*Just wait until everyone's gone, then you can go over there,*" I whispered back.

Unfortunately, Mr. Christianson didn't agree with my idea of waiting for the parking lot to clear out of all humans before his daughter got in the van. He got out of the Langstermobile and looked directly over to where Rivka was trying to hide behind the wall of Royal Rulers bodies. In his most-embarrassing father bark he bellowed, "COME ON, RIVKA! LET'S GO!"

Now if he hollered the name "Jessica" or "Samantha" it could have been a dozen different girls he was calling for, but there was only *one* Rivka in the whole school and all eyes in the parking lot turned to her. Even though she was practically crouching already, it seemed she shrunk about five more inches.

Natalie turned around and looked at Rivka. *"That's* your father's car?"

"Well...not exactly...," Rivka stammered, as she slowly straightened up. "It's a company car."

"Your father works for a motel?" Hailey asked.

Before Rivka could answer, Natalie said to the other Royal Rulers, "Hey, remember Megan McManus?"

"Yes! Motel McManus!" Cassandra said. "Her father used to manage a motel and she even used to live there."

Natalie looked at Rivka. "Don't tell me you live in a motel, Goober."

Rivka looked at me, and in her eyes, I saw the fear of a trapped animal.

Lie, Rivka! Remember our solemn hope-to-die oath we made.

"Well?" Natalie pressed. "Are you a motel kid, Goober?"

Rivka silently begged me to help.

Please don't bring me into this, I silently begged back.

"COME ON, RIVKA!" Mr. Christianson yelled again from the Langstermobile. "WE'RE GOING TO BE LATE!"

Without answering Natalie, Rivka slunk her way over to the Langstermobile with a parking lot full of kids watching. She got in the Langstermobile and as it drove away, I swear I saw her broken spirit jump out of the van and disappear into the bushes.

Natalie turned to me. "You must know...does Goober live in a motel?"

Natalie, Phoebe, and what felt like a thousand other kids stared at me. Sheesh, didn't anyone have a bus to catch or anything?

"Well...I've never actually been to her house," I stammered.

It wasn't a complete lie. I never actually did go to Rivka's *house*. True, I had been to her apartment at the motel, but we could overlook that little technicality.

"Besides," I added, "just because her father drives a motel van doesn't mean she lives there, does it?" It was a feeble attempt, but I knew there was no pulling the casket out of the grave now that they'd all seen the Langstermoble. I quickly mumbled something about my bus leaving soon and hurried away.

On the bus ride home, I overheard kids talking about the insanely ugly van that Rivka had been picked up in. As we drove by the motel, one of Aaron's friends pointed out that the sign on top of the van had also read Langster Motel. Rivka's cover was blown. And just by process of association, I knew it was only a matter of time before everyone found out I lived there too.

When Rivka got home from her dentist appointment, we sat on the back steps together. "So...what did everyone say after I left?"

"Everyone had to run to catch their buses. I don't think anyone really gave it a second thought."

"Are you kidding? Didn't you see the faces of the angry villagers when they spotted the Langstermobile?"

"It wasn't that bad," I lied.

"That's easy for you to say. You didn't have to ride in it with the entire school watching."

She was right. If it had been me, and my mother had picked me up in the Langstermobile with everyone watching, I would just drop out of school right now.

The next day in science, Natalie turned around to me.

I automatically handed her the extra homework sheet I had done for her.

"So?" she sat there staring at me.

"What? Didn't I do all the homework we were supposed to?"

"No, not that. What's the story about Goober and that hearse that picked her up yesterday?"

I felt my face reddening and before I could stutter out some stupid answer, our science teacher came in the room and told everyone to settle down. Natalie had no choice but to turn around. I was saved once again from having to answer her.

When class ended and our teacher asked for a volunteer to take a note to the office, I raised my hand. Sometimes it's hard to shake all the teacher's-pet traits out of you. By the time I got to the cafeteria and bought my lunch, all the Royal Rulers were already sitting at their usual table. Rivka wasn't there. She was sitting with Monica and Bernice. When I waved her over, Rivka shook her head and stayed where she was.

At lunch no one even brought up the topic of the Langstermobile—or Rivka for that matter. Mostly Natalie, Cassandra, and Hailey flirted with Anthony DeFranco, Jake Pellechino, and Jonathon Parker who pulled up some chairs and joined our table halfway through lunch. Phoebe paid no attention to anyone at the table. She was busy looking at and hiding her cell phone from the lunch monitors. I spent the lunch period mostly nodding and smiling, and wondering if this was how it felt to be popular.

"How come you didn't sit with us lunch?" I asked Rivka later on the bus.

"Because when I went to sit at the Royal Rulers' table, they snubbed me."

"How? What did they say?"

"Natalie made a comment about how maybe I should sit with my own kind."

"She didn't!"

"She did!"

"Just because Natalie made a comment didn't mean they all snubbed you, Rivka."

"Well, none of the others came to my defense," Rivka said. "I guess they think I'm not worthy enough for their group."

"Natalie was probably just joking around. Don't let her comment get to you, okay?"

"They're a bunch of snobs who are using you for a free homework pass, Cali."

"If you think about it, in a way we're using them too."

"Well, I'm done with it," Rivka said.

The next day in the cafeteria, Rivka and I bought our lunches and when we went to sit down, I headed towards the Royal Rulers' table.

"Cali, where are you going?" Rivka asked.

"Come on. We're not going down without a fight."

"No," she said stopping in the middle of the cafeteria. "I'm not letting them humiliate me again."

"Come on, Rivka. This is our future we're talking about," I said.

Rivka shook her head. "I'm going over and sitting with Monica and Bernice. You coming?"

"Will you hate me if I don't?"

She shrugged. "Do whatever you want." She walked away.

Even though I didn't feel good about it, I headed over to the Royal Ruler table that was currently surrounded by boys.

On the bus ride home Rivka was unusually quiet.

"You mad at me?" I asked.

"No, but I'm not happy that you picked the Royal Rulers over me."

"You're the one who chose to sit with Monica and Bernice."

"That's because I was told I wasn't wanted at the Royal Rulers' table."

"I really think you're imagining things, Rivka."

But I knew she wasn't because at the lunch table when the Royals were making plans to go to Natalie's house on Saturday, Natalie said to me, "And for the love of chocolate, Cali, if you come, don't bring Goober with you."

Chapter 22

After my long walk back to the motel from the bus stop, I went straight to my room, with a quick wave to Rivka, who was already watching the Hudson boys and the two Jones girls. My mother was sitting on her bed hunched over a laptop. A partially empty McDonald's bag sat next to her and a couple of stray French fries were on the bed, including a squished up one she was half sitting on.

"Mom, can I go to Natalie's house on Saturday?" I asked, tossing my backpack on the dresser and sitting down on the bed beside her. Mom kept typing and didn't even look up.

I reached over and nudged her. "Mom?"

"I'm busy Cali," she replied, clicking the mouse a few times.

"Can I go to Natalie's house Saturday afternoon?" I asked again.

When my mother didn't answer, I said a little louder, "Mom! Can I go?"

She nodded absently, as she furiously hit the letters on her keyboard.

"Will you give me a ride there? She lives on Reston Road."

"Uh-huh," she said, as she continued typing.

"I want to be there for one o'clock, okay?"

Mom looked up at me, annoyed. "Cali, I really need to finish this article for the newspaper or they're not going to pay me for it."

I knew better than to bother Mom when she was working, but distraction was usually the best way to get a yes.

The next morning, Rivka knocked on my door. "My mother is driving Shannon and Phoenix to the movies on Saturday," she informed me. "Want to go with them?"

"I can't," I told her.

"I can loan you the money if your Mom won't give you any," she offered.

"I'm kind of busy on Saturday." I tried to sound like it was no big deal, but Rivka knows I never do anything on the weekend but homework and babysit and I wouldn't give up any trip away from the motel for either of those.

"Busy doing what?" she asked.

Do you know how hard it is to tell your best friend you're getting together with other friends and she wasn't invited? Well, I certainly didn't know how. I just stood there like a doofus trying to come up with an excuse why I couldn't go with her.

"So? What are you busy doing?" Rivka pressed.

"The truth?" I asked.

"Of course, I want the truth."

"I'm getting together with the Royal Rulers."

"...and I'm not invited, right?"

"Rivka...I really want to go with them," I pleaded, hoping she'd understand.

"So now you're a Royal Ruler and I'm a nobody. I guess you don't need me any longer now that you're part of the in-crowd."

"No...Rivka... you're still my best friend."

"You sure have a funny way of showing it. You won't wait for the bus with me in the morning, you won't get off the bus at the motel with me in the afternoon, and now you won't sit with me at lunch."

"You're the one who won't sit with me at lunch," I said.

"No, I won't sit with the Royal Rulers because they don't want me at their table. And now you are ashamed to be seen with me."

"Rivka...it's not that..."

"That's exactly it! You're afraid if you hang around with me, kids will start treating you the same way they're treating me."

"I'm not ashamed to be seen with you. I'm just ashamed of living here."

"Living here is part of who we are, Cali. I'm not going to hide it anymore and you shouldn't either."

"No! Do you know what the kids at school will do if they find out?"

"Umm...maybe treat us the same way they're treating me now since everyone already knows about me anyway?"

"They'll start calling us the motel kids like they do with the elementary school kids. Or even worse, they'll call us homeless people."

"We're not homeless. We have homes."

"You at least live in an apartment, Rivka. But, me? Do you know what people will say when they find out I live in a motel room?"

"They'll say you live in a motel room. So what?"

"You made a promise not to tell anyone, remember?"

"Well, I'm tired of hiding it all the time at school. I'm going to tell Bernice and Monica I live here. I promise I won't even mention you when I tell them."

"They'll figure it out, Rivka! Once they know about you, they'll figure out I live here too!"

"I'm tired of all the lying and pretending, Cali. I'm not going to do it anymore."

"Fine! But once you tell people, you're on your own. Don't come running to me to try to fix things for you."

"Fix things for me?" Rivka stared at me in disbelief. "All you've done is mess things up."

I stared back. "What do you mean by that?"

"You were so intent on us trying to impress Phoebe and Natalie, and all the Royal Rulers, I couldn't even be myself anymore. Anytime I tried to act normal, you gave me the evil eye."

"I did not!"

"You did too! Maybe you're happy acting all fake, but I'm tired of trying to be someone I'm not."

"I'm not acting like someone I'm not!" I cried.

"Well, if this is who you really are, then you're just as stuck up as Phoebe and Natalie and all the others."

"If that's the way you think, then maybe you don't deserve to be a Royal Ruler."

"And maybe you DO deserve to be one. You're just like them."

"Fine! Stay a goober your whole life!" I snapped.

"At least goobers are honest about who they are," she snapped back. "If it takes having to do other people's homework and acting all stuck up and fake to be popular, then it obviously isn't for me. If people don't like me because of how I dress, or how curly my hair is, or where I live, they aren't people I want to hang out with!"

"Go ahead and commit social suicide if you want, Rivka. But you better not take me down with you. If you even hint to anyone that I live here, I'll never talk to you again!"

"Why don't you just start now...don't ever talk to me again!"

"FINE!" I yelled.

For the next couple of days, Rivka and I pretended the other person didn't exit. We didn't talk at school, and we didn't talk to each other at the motel after school. Most of the time I stayed in my room, doing mine and Natalie's and Cassandra's homework. At school, I'd sit with the Royal Rulers during lunch, and she'd sit with Monica and Bernice. When the three of them walked by our table, I'd be sure to be looking anywhere other than where they were.

"You and Goober have a fight or something?" Phoebe asked after the third day of our silent treatment with each other.

"We're both just taking some space right now," I said.

Natalie was checking her makeup in a compact mirror. "She wasn't in our league anyway," she said, looking up. "I mean, the way she dresses, it's like she just came off the farm or something."

"What is it with you?" Phoebe cut in. "Why is it always about what people wear or what they have? Not everyone is rich you know, Natalie."

Natalie looked surprised. "What? Now you're suddenly into charity cases?"

"Just lay off her," Phoebe said, throwing her head in Rivka's direction.

"Since when did you get a soft spot for misfits?" Natalie stared in disbelief at Phoebe, and the rest of us stared in disbelief at both of them.

"I said, lay off!" Phoebe snapped at her.

Wow! Phoebe was totally defending Rivka against Natalie. And the sad part was, I couldn't even tell Rivka about it.

Chapter 23

Saturday afternoon I was in the room getting ready to go to Natalie's house, dodging around Mom who was getting ready too. At least I thought she was getting ready to take me to Natalie's until she said, "Mrs. Jones and I have some errands to run. I told her you'd watch her kids while we're gone."

"What? No! You're supposed to drive me to Natalie's house today."

"Who's Natalie?"

"My friend from school. Remember? I asked you days ago if I could go to her house."

"When did you ask?"

"When I first came home from school. When you were working on your article."

"You know I get so absorbed in what I'm doing, I don't pay attention when people talk to me."

"But you said I could go! You said you'd give me a ride, and I already told the girls I was going!"

"Mrs. Jones and I won't be more than an hour or two and when we get back, I'll drive you over to your friend's house."

I stormed outside, and plopped myself down in the side yard where I could see Trinika and Delilah playing in the sandbox. Hakeem wasn't anywhere in sight, but for all I cared, he could stay wherever he was. Rivka was sitting nearby watching the three Hudson boys. At first we didn't say anything to each other, but finally I grumbled hello to her.

"I thought you were hanging out with the Royal Rulers today," she said.

"So did I, but once again, knowing how much I love watching kids for free, my mother volunteered my services to watch the Jones kids."

Rivka picked up a stick and started doodling in the dirt. "I guess I could watch them. I'm stuck here anyway."

"Thanks, but I don't have a ride now."
"Where are you supposed to meet them?"
"At Natalie's house. On Reston Road."
"Reston Road has some nice houses."
"Yeah, too bad I won't be seeing them."
"You can take the bus there."
"I wouldn't know how."
"You catch the city bus up the road on the corner of Route 9 and Wilson Street, then you take it straight up Wilson to Division Street which is only a block away from Reston Road."

"How do you even know that?" I asked.
"I'm psychic, remember?"
"I'm supposed to base the bus route on your psychic ability?"

She smirked a little. "Actually, Shannon pet sits for a family that lives on Reston."

"Are you really okay watching the Jones kids for me?" I asked.

"It's not like I have anything better to do."
"You sure? You absolutely sure?"

"Go! I know how bad you want the Royals to like you. Besides, I'm dying to hear what Natalie's house looks like."

"Thanks, Rivka. I'll owe you one."

I ran to my room, brushed my hair, put on some lip gloss, and I was off to try to figure out how to get a bus to Natalie's house.

Walking down Route 9, I checked each road sign for Wilson Street, but after a few blocks I started wondering if I was going the wrong direction. My shoes were pinching my feet, and I was wilting from the sun beating down on me.

Michael Fitzpatrick drove by in his parents' car. He spotted me in the rearview mirror as he passed me, so quickly pulled over. I hurried up to the car.

"Where you headed?" he asked, leaning over to the passenger's side window.

"I'm going to my friend's house. I'm trying to find where to catch the bus that goes near Reston Road," I explained.

"Want a ride?" Michael asked.

"To the bus stop?"

"No, to your friend's house."

"Seriously?"

He nodded and reached over to open the door.

"You're a lifesaver again, Michael," I said getting in. "I had no idea the bus stop was this far from the motel."

"So, how do I get to Reston Road?" he asked.

"Do you have a cell phone we can use to get directions?"

"Nope, I'm the last hold out on the planet. No cell phone."

"I don't have one either. Not holding out—just don't have the money for one."

I told Michael how Rivka told me to catch the bus on the corner of Wilson and get off on Division Street. "She said Reston Road was only a block from there."

"Oh...I know how to get to Division," Michael said, taking a sudden right turn.

Once we were on Division Street, we started checking every street sign for Reston Road. "There!" I shouted when I spotted the sign.

We drove slowly down Reston Road and I couldn't help wondering how a city with a loser motel like the one I lived in also had a gorgeous neighborhood like the one we were driving through. Michael drove slowly until we came to the house number Natalie had written on a cafeteria napkin for me. He let out a low whistle as the two of us stared at the mega-mansion where Natalie lived. Her house was bigger than all of Langster Motel. Rivka's early prediction of Natalie being rich was dead on. If Natalie had a white Persian cat or a honey-colored Pomeranian like Rivka figured, I would totally believe every prediction she told me from then on.

"I'm only about a half hour late, I said unstrapping my seat belt to get out. "Hopefully, they didn't decide to ditch me and go somewhere else."

"You need a ride home later?" Michael asked.

"I'll just catch the bus," I said. "That is, if I can find it."

"I can come back to get you in a few hours if you want."

"Really? You'd do that?"

"It's not like I have anything else to do," Michael said.

I guess living in the motel meant he didn't have much of a life either.

"That's really nice of you," I said.

Just then the front door opened and Natalie, Cassandra, and Hailey came bounding out of the house and over to the car.

Natalie went over to Michael's side of the car and stuck her face in his open window. "Look what the California girl brought us," Natalie said, in high flirt mode. "You are staying, aren't you?"

Michael shook his head, then revved the car's engine, signifying his desire to hurry up and leave.

Cassandra and Hailey were standing behind Natalie. "Come on, stay!" they both pleaded.

Michael ignored them and turned to me, "What time do you want me to pick you up?"

I looked at Natalie for the answer.

"Why don't you stay, then you don't have to worry what time to come back," she said to Michael.

Again, he shook his head.

"Well, if you must go, come back about 4:00—unless, of course, you want to come back sooner and hang out with us awhile?" She smiled sweetly at Michael.

Michael put the car in gear, signaling Natalie to back away.

After he drove off, I followed the girls inside. The foyer in Natalie's house was about the size of four motel rooms. There were two large arched doorways on each side of the front door leading to a formal living room on one side and an elegant dining room on the other. There was a wide carpeted stairway in the middle of the foyer which led up to the second floor, and a third arched doorway behind the stairs that lead to another section of the house. I followed the three girls as they went through the arch of the middle doorway, down a hall, and into what Natalie called the Great Room. It was a room about the size of our school gym with a two-story high ceiling with eight skylights.

A large television hanging on the wall displayed eight different locations around the outside of Natalie's house. Security cameras. I guessed that was why the three girls came out when we arrived. They must have seen Michael's car drive up.

Phoebe was sprawled across a black leather chair staring at the screen on her cell phone. I said hello to her, but she didn't respond. If I actually owned a cell phone, I could have texted "hello" to her and I might have gotten a text answer back. Haley, Cassandra, and Natalie plopped down on the white leather sofa and started digging into a spread of snacks that had been put out on the glass coffee table—potato chips, a bowl of popcorn, a platter of cut up fresh vegetables, cut up fruit, and a plate of home baked cookies.

"Help yourself to a drink," Natalie said, pointing to a refrigerator on the other side of the room. It was stuffed with cans of soda, bottles of juices, and water. I pulled out a bottle of water and sat down in an overstuffed leather chair next to the sofa.

"I am so sick of school," Cassandra said dramatically.

"I know, I can barely keep up with all the homework," Hailey whined.

Hello? How about poor me who could barely keep up with doing my own work, no less Natalie's science homework, and Cassandra's math homework? Did they not realize how much time that took?

"Anyone start their speech yet?" Natalie asked.

Uh-oh. I had a suspicion that's why I was invited here. She was going to ask me to write her speech for her. I had already finished my own, but there was no way I could do hers. *Please don't ask! Please don't ask!* I tried to will her request away.

Before Natalie had a chance to say anything more, Phoebe broke in. "Are you guys going to watch a movie or what?"

Thank you, Phoebe! After a five-minute argument over which movie to watch, Natalie finally clicked a title on the television menu without waiting for everyone to agree on it. Then she, Hailey, and Cassandra talked throughout the movie, so I missed parts and had a hard time following it. Phoebe didn't even bother watching it. She was busy playing games on her cell phone.

When the movie ended, Natalie and Hailey stood up to stretch. They then gave Cassandra a nudge and all three girls turned and looked at me. *Oh, no! Here comes the "do my speech for me" speech.*

"Cali," Natalie began. "We need to talk."

It's a known fact that it's never good when someone starts off with, "We need to talk."

Cassandra took over. "We like you and all, but…"

"…but we have an image to uphold," Natalie continued.

"*Oh.*" It was all I could think of to say.

"Yeah, in case you haven't noticed, we're pretty popular," Hailey said. "Aren't we, girls?" She looked around waiting for everyone to confirm, but no one bothered to answer her.

"So, anyway," continued Natalie, ignoring Hailey, "if you want to be one of us, you can't be hanging around with kids like Goober."

"You mean Rivka?" I looked at each of them.

"Duh!" Natalie answered.

"Yeah, we don't want her ruining our image," Cassandra added.

I sat there stunned. Were they actually telling me I couldn't be one of the Royals if I was friends with Rivka?

"As long as you're okay with that, then we're good," Natalie finished.

To have someone tell me I couldn't be friends with them if I wanted to be friends with someone else was pretty gutsy. Sure, Rivka and I were kind of mad at each other right now, but it was only thanks to her offering to watch the kids I was supposed to be watching that I could even be here today. Maybe she wasn't really that mad at me. Could I give up being friends with her in order to hang with these girls who everyone at school was in awe of? Being popular meant having plenty of friends, so if I traded one friend for a whole bunch more, wasn't I getting the better of the deal?

The three girls sat there waiting for me to answer. Phoebe was still staring at her cell phone, but she had stopped playing her game and I think she was waiting to hear my answer too. Rivka was my best friend. To not be friends with her because the Royals told me not to was not right, but instead of telling them so, I answered in a tiny voice, "Okay..."

Chapter 24

After I had agreed to separate myself from Rivka for the sake of the group's image, Natalie, Cassandra, and Hailey spent the rest of the afternoon arguing about which boys at school they thought were the cutest ones. Instead of keeping up with their conversation, I kept thinking about Rivka and wondering if I really was prepared to end our friendship. Of course, it would be hard to ignore her around the motel, but did I really want to separate myself from her at school?

About ten minutes to four, I stood up and announced that I was going to wait outside for my ride.

It surprised me when Natalie offered to walk me out, but I found out why when we got to the front door. "So, what's the story with this Michael guy?" she asked.

"What do you mean?"

"He's always giving you rides."

This was only the second time it happened, but we could overlook that technicality.

"He's a friend," I said. "He lives near me."

"Are you...like going together?" Natalie asked.

"Me? Going with Michael?" It was so far-fetched I almost laughed, but I caught myself and just shook my head.

"Well, if you're not going with him, can you fix me up with him?"

"You do realize he's 17."

"So?"

"I don't think he'd go for someone our age."

"Girls are so much more mature than boys, so he and I are practically the same age in maturity level."

"Well...yeah...but..."

"See what you can do for me, okay?" She handed me a slip of paper with her cell phone number on it. "Give this to him, and I'll owe you big time," she said handing me the paper.

Natalie stayed outside with me until Michael drove up. She waved to him, but Michael didn't bother to wave back.

On the ride home, I waited a few moments before I blurted out, "Natalie likes you."

Michael just stared at the road.

"She wanted me to give you her phone number," I said, fiddling around with the piece of paper with Natalie's number on it.

"Is she the girl claiming to be older than she really is?"

"Yeah, that's her."

"She's a little young for me," he said.

"Yeah, I told Natalie you wouldn't go out with a 13-year-old." I crumpled up the paper in my hand.

"Besides, I like someone else," Michael said.

"You have a girlfriend?" I sounded more shocked than I meant to.

"Not a girlfriend. I like someone, only she doesn't know I like her."

"She doesn't know? You haven't even dropped hints when you talk to her?"

"In case you haven't noticed, I'm not very good at talking to girls."

"But, you're talking pretty good to me right now."

"You're more like a kid, than a girl."

"Gee, thanks."

"No offense," he said.

"I'm no expert, Michael...I've never even had a boyfriend before...but why don't you try telling the girl that you like her? If she tells you she's not interested, at least you'll know and can move on."

"That's what I'm afraid of--that she's not interested in me and then I'd be too embarrassed to even look at her after that."

"You won't know until you ask."

Michael drove a few miles, then glanced over at me. "Would you ask her for me?"

I stared at him in disbelief. "Me? Talk to a girl for you?"

"Yeah. You know her better than I do."

"Know who?"

"Your sister."

"My sister! You mean Phoenix?" If I wasn't sitting down, I probably would have fallen down, that's how shocked I was. "You like Phoenix?"

He turned bright red. "Uh-huh."

"Why haven't you told her? Don't you realize how much she's crushing on you?"

"What? ...She is?" Michael glanced over at me to see if I was serious.

"How could you not see it?" I stared at him to see if he really was that thick. "Phoenix has wanted to go out with you since the first time she laid eyes on you."

"Really? You're not just saying that?"

"I'm dead serious!"

"So, if I asked her to go out with me, do you think she'd say yes?"

"You could ask her to marry you and she'd probably say yes!"

"Whoa...I don't know about marriage," he said, as a slow grin crept across his face.

"Okay, maybe hold off on the marriage thing. But definitely ask her out. I promise you, she won't say no."

His grin got bigger. It was the first time I ever saw Michael Fitzpatrick look happy. By the time we got to the motel, he looked like a different person.

As soon as we pulled into the parking lot, I noticed kids running around all crazy—crazier than normal. As soon as Michael parked, Hakeem came running over to the car. "We can't find Trinika," he cried.

"What do you mean, you can't find her?" I asked, getting out.

Hakeem had to catch his breath before he continued. "She was in the sandbox, but she disappeared."

"She couldn't have just disappeared. Where's Rivka?" I asked, looking over at the side yard.

"She's around back looking for Trini."

As soon as he said that, Rivka came from behind the motel. Her eyes were wide, and her hair was more wild than normal. "We can't find Trinika anywhere," she said.

"How long has she been missing?" I asked.

"About twenty minutes. Hakeem was watching his sisters for me for a few minutes while I went inside to use the bathroom," Rivka explained.

Hakeem picked up the story. "Yeah, and when she went inside, Delilah fell off the swing, and was crying, and I was trying to get her to stop."

"While he was taking care of Delilah, Trinika must have wandered off," Rivka finished.

"Did you check inside the boys' clubhouse?" I asked.

"I just looked," Rivka said. "She's not there."

"Did you check your apartment to see if Pauly's holding her hostage?"

"Yeah, she wasn't there," Rivka said.

"How about your room?" I asked Hakeem.

"She wasn't there either," he said, fighting to hold back tears.

Michael spoke up for the first time since getting out of the car. "How about the other motel rooms?" he asked quietly "Have you checked them all?"

"Not yet," Rivka said.

"Yeah, maybe she decided to go visit someone," I said. "Hakeem, go knock on the Azars' door and see if she's playing with Reza or Isabella."

"I'll check the Riveras' room to make sure Hector or Roberto don't have her tied up in there," Rivka said.

"She's got to be around here somewhere," I said. "I'll go check with Jodi."

"I'll go see if my parents have seen her," Michael said.

I headed over to Jodi's room and stuck my head in the open door. Jodi was changing the baby's diaper on one of the beds, and judging by the smell coming from the room, it was a nasty one.

"By any chance is Trinika Jones here?" I asked, covering my nose to keep from gagging.

Jodi counted the heads bouncing around her room. "Nope, unfortunately, these all belong to me," she said, seemingly unaffected by the smell of the poopy diaper.

"Trinika wandered off, and we're checking all the rooms to see if she's in any of them."

"Boys, do you know where Trini is?" she asked the three kids zooming their Matchbox cars all over the room.

Her boys didn't seem to care about the poopy diaper smell either, and they didn't seem to hear their mother when she talked to them.

"I asked if you have seen Trini," Jodi asked again. All three boys shook their heads and continued running their vehicles all over the room. I hurried back outside for some fresh air.

I met up with Michael and his parents.

"Michael said Trinika Jones is missing," Mrs. Fitzpatrick said. "Did anyone check the boy's clubhouse in the back?"

I nodded. "Rivka already did, but no luck there."

"I'll go check again," Mr. Fitzpatrick said. "Maybe she's hiding behind it or somewhere around it where Rivka hadn't looked."

"I'll look around the side yard," Mrs. Fitzpatrick said. "Michael used to hide in bushes all the time when he was little. Maybe that's what she's doing."

Michael's face turned pink.

"I'll make sure she's not in our room," I said.

Georgia, Stacey, Gabby, Isabella, and the new girl Anita Sullivan were playing Old Maid on one of the beds.

"Anybody see Trinika Jones?" I asked.

"I saw her yesterday," Georgia said as she pulled a card out of the ones Isabella's was offering from her hands.

"I mean, like in the last twenty minutes."

"Nope," Stacey said.

Gabby, Anita, and Isabella shook their heads.

"She's missing," I told them. "We can't find her anywhere."

"She's probably in the boys' clubhouse," Stacey said, matter-of-factly.

"Rivka looked there already, but Mr. Fitzpatrick is looking again. Any other places you can think of where she might be?"

"Nope," Stacey said.

Georgia looked at her friends. "Let's help look for her," she said.

All the girls dropped their cards on the bed and followed me outside.

The Azars were just coming out of their room, and the parking lot was filling up with motel residents.

"Hakeem says Trini missing?" Mrs. Azar said.

"Yeah, we can't find her anywhere," Rivka said, coming up with Mrs. Rivera behind her.

"She maybe with her mama?" Mrs. Azar suggested.

"No, Mrs. Jones went out with my mom," I said. "She doesn't even know Trinika's missing yet." I didn't mention how my mother's and Mrs. Jones' quick lunch was now running into the dinner hour.

"*Yu* look in rec room?" Mrs. Azar asked.

"I didn't," Rivka said. "I don't know if anyone else did."

"We look there," Mrs. Azar said. "Come! Come!" she instructed her husband, and the two of them scurried over to the rec room.

Rivka's parents came out of the Christiansons' apartment, along with Shannon and Phoenix.

"She couldn't have wandered too far," Mrs. Christianson said, having already heard that Trinika was missing. "She knows not to go in the road, right, Hakeem?"

Hakeem nodded.

"If she's hiding around here, she better come out now," Mr. Christianson said. Then he called for her with his booming voice, "TRINIKA!!"

"Dad! You're going to scare her if you yell like that," Shannon warned.

Ignoring her, Mr. Christianson yelled Trinika's name a few more times.

Soon everyone at the motel was involved in the search. Both adults and kids were checking every bush, every room, every hiding place looking for the lost girl.

"*Trinika! Trinika!*" echoed all over the parking lot, the side yard, and the back of the motel, even inside the Langstermobile, but Trinika Jones was nowhere to be found.

By the time Mom and Mrs. Jones pulled in, Trinika had been missing over an hour. As soon as Mom and Mrs. Jones got out of the car, Mrs. Christianson and Mrs. Fitzpatrick went over to them to tell them the news, and the rest of us followed behind.

"Oh, Lordie! My sweet baby!" Mrs. Jones cried, falling into Mrs. Christianson arms.

"I'm sure she's fine," Mrs. Christianson tried to comfort Mrs. Jones. "She probably fell asleep somewhere."

Rivka said to Mrs. Jones, "I left Hakeem in charge for only a few minutes, but by the time I came back outside from using the bathroom she had already wandered off."

"Cali, why weren't you watching her?" Mom asked.

Everyone looked over at me, and I felt prickly heat fill my face and body. "I was at Natalie's house," I said.

"What?" Mom's eyes got angry. "You were supposed to watch the Jones kids until we got back!"

I waited for Rivka to jump in and admit she had offered to watch the kids for me, but she just stood there looking at the ground.

"You disobeyed me and left the motel when you were supposed to be watching the kids. Now look what happened," Mom scolded.

"I'm sorry, Mom. I didn't think it would be a big deal if I went."

Mrs. Christianson jumped in and rescued me from further public humiliation. "The police have already been called, so they should be here soon. In the meantime, we should all spread out and keep looking for her."

"Has anyone checked the woods behind the motel yet?" Mr. Fitzpatrick asked.

"She's scared of the woods," Hakeem said. "She'd never go in there."

"We should check anyway." Mr. Fitzpatrick turned to Mr. Christianson, "Let's go take a look."

"I'll go with you too," Michael, volunteered.

A quiet voice came from the back of the crowd, "I go too." It was Mr. Azar. It was the first time I ever heard him speak.

As the four of them headed towards the woods, Delilah started crying, blubbering something about Trinika getting eaten alive by coyotes.

"Oh, sweetheart. There are no coyotes around here," Mrs. Fitzpatrick said, picking her up to comfort her.

"But Rivka said..." Delilah whimpered.

Mrs. Jones looked about ready to collapse, so Mrs. Azar hurried over with a chair for her to sit in. "You not worry," she said, patting Mrs. Jones' hand. "We find her."

"Have all the rooms been checked?" Mom asked.

"Yeah, we checked them all," Rivka answered.

"Not all of them," Hakeem piped up. "No one checked Old Man Malcolm's room."

"You mean no one asked him if he saw Trini?" Mrs. Jones looked around the group.

"He may have seen her wander off," Mrs. Christianson added.

"No one wants to talk to him," Pauly Christianson piped up. "He's creepy."

"Why are you kids so afraid of him?" Mom asked. "He's a lonely old man, not a serial killer."

"That's right," Mrs. Christianson said. "I don't know who started those ridiculous rumors about him."

Rivka and I snuck a peek at each other, then quickly looked away.

"Old Man Malcolm was right there when Trinika disappeared," Hakeem said, pointing over to where Malcolm was sitting outside his room. "I bet anything he knows what happened to her."

"He's been watching everyone look for her, but hasn't even offered to help," Rivka added.

"Well, let's go ask him," Mom said to Mrs. Rivera and Mrs. Christianson. The moms headed towards Old Man Malcolm's room. All the kids followed them.

"Malcolm, Trinika Jones is missing and no one can find her," Mrs. Christianson said to the old man sitting in the chair.

"Yeah, I figured something was up," the old man replied.

"Did you see her playing on the playground earlier?"

"No, Ma'am. I didn't see her."

"So, you didn't see her wander off?"

"No, Ma'am."

"Or notice a stranger hanging around maybe?" Mrs. Christianson kept pressing.

"No, Ma'am. I didn't see anything."

"You had to have seen her," Hakeem exploded. "You were watching us the whole time!"

Old Man Malcolm turned towards him. "While it may appear that way, the truth is I can't see very much. Lost most of my sight back during the Korean War thanks to some shrapnel that decided to make its home in my face. Ever since, I've been legally blind."

"If you're so blind, how come you bent down and picked up a ball earlier when Trinika kicked it by you?" Hakeem asked.

"I can see a little, but only about a foot in front of me. Anything beyond that, I can't see."

"We had no idea, Malcolm," Mrs. Christianson said. "You never said anything about it before."

"Nope, don't want anyone pitying me," he said.

We headed back to where Mrs. Jones was sitting being comforted by Mrs. Azar and Mrs. Fitzpatrick. She was sobbing, "My poor baby," over and over.

I couldn't stand seeing her like that, and I couldn't stand feeling like this whole thing would have never happened if I hadn't gone to Natalie's house. It wasn't Rivka's or Hakeem's fault Trinika was missing. It was mine. In spite of my acting like Trinika was nothing but a pain, I cared about her. I cared about her a lot. If anything bad happened to her, I would hate myself more than I already did. I left the group in the parking lot and headed towards the woods. Unless she was abducted by a stranger or aliens in a spaceship, the woods seemed the most logical place she'd be.

The farther away from the motel I got, the thicker the trees became. I could hear the other searchers calling out Trinika's name, but couldn't see them at all. I headed away from the direction of their voices. When I could barely hear them, I began calling her name out too. "Trinika! Can you hear me?"

I heard plenty of noise in the woods—birds chirping and chattering, traffic in the distance from Route 9, but no little girl shouting back.

As I walked, I was searching the area around me for signs of Trinika having been through this area, hoping she had dropped a toy or a baby blanket or some clue like they always do in the movies, but I didn't see anything like that.

I must have been searching for a half hour calling out her name when I finally heard a faint voice cry back, "I'm here!"

I rushed in the direction of the voice. "Trinika, where are you?" I yelled out again.

"Here! I'm over here!"

"Keep shouting so I can find you."

And she kept repeating, "I'm here," every time I yelled her name. Finally, I spotted her sitting on a large rock, her face streaked with dirty trails made from tears. Her hair had leaves and sticks in it, and she looked like a baby swamp monster. She was the best swamp monster I could've ever hoped to run into.

I ran up to her and she threw her arms around me. I held her tight to me and could feel her little heart pounding against mine.

"You had everyone worried, you know," I said to her, petting her dirty hair.

"I was so scared," she cried.

"You're safe, now," I said. "What made you come here? In the woods?"

"I wanted to pet the doggie. He ran into the woods and when I went to look for him, I got lost."

"Well, let's get you back to your mother," I said, picking the little swamp monster up.

As I walked through the woods carrying Trinika in my arms, I called out, "I FOUND HER! I FOUND TRINIKA!" As soon as they heard me shouting, Mr. Christianson, Mr. Fitzpatrick, Mr. Azar and Michael all came hurrying from the other side of the woods.

"Here, let me take her," Mr. Christianson said to me, reaching to take Trinika from my arms.

Trinika wrapped her arms and legs around me tighter. "No, I want Cali to carry me."

"But you're such a big girl," Mr. Fitzpatrick said to her. "You're too heavy for Cali to carry all the way back to the motel."

"It's okay," I said to him. "I got her."

As we made our way through the woods and around the back of the motel with Mr. Christianson shouting the good news in front of us, everyone from the motel hurried to meet us, including a couple of police officers who had answered the missing child call.

Now for the record, Mrs. Jones isn't a particularly loud person, but she let out a scream louder than a freight train's whistle when she saw her daughter. She rushed towards us quicker than I ever saw her move before.

"OH, MY BABY!" she shouted as she snatched Trinika out of my arms.

"She followed a dog into the woods and got lost," I tried to explain, but I don't think Mrs. Jones heard me.

She was clutching Trinika tightly, rocking back and forth and sobbing her thanks to the supreme god of lost children. Trinika looked like she was being smothered by her mother's body, and I wanted to rescue her (again) so she could at least breathe. Delilah was jumping up and down beside them shouting, "The coyotes didn't get her! The coyotes didn't get her!"

After all the excitement died down and the police left, the kids went back to playing on the swings and in the sandbox. The adults brought chairs outside and sat in the parking lot talking and, I'm happy to report, watching their own kids for a change.

Chapter 25

Sunday afternoon I stayed in my room practicing my English speech, which was due in a few more days. My mother and sisters were all out, so I had the room to myself.

I stood in front of the dresser mirror and said to my reflection, "I bet you didn't know I am a middle child..."

It sounded lame.

"I bet you didn't *KNOW* I am a middle child..."

Over and over I repeated it, trying out different ways of saying it, using different voices, different word stresses, and different facial movements. I even tried it with a British accent, but it didn't help. No matter how I said it, it was boring. There had to be something about me that was more interesting than being a middle child.

The door to the room opened, and Phoenix came in.

"Hey, what do you think is interesting about me?" I asked.

"Nothing." She went into the kitchenette area and opened the door to the small refrigerator.

"Come on, Phoenix...I really need some help."

"Why do you want to know what's interesting about you?" She grabbed a can of soda and popped the tab open.

"I have to give a speech in English on Wednesday. It has to start out, 'I bet you didn't know...' and then I have to tell something about myself that is different or unique, or interesting."

"It's due on Wednesday and you're just starting to think about it now? That's not like you." She took a long gulp of soda and put the opened can back in the refrigerator.

"Well, I wrote a speech already, but I'm not happy with how it sounds." I handed her my middle child speech.

Phoenix read it, then started making snoring sounds. I threw a pillow at her. "It's not that bad!" I cried, knowing full well it was.

"Why don't you tell about what it was like living in New Jersey," she said.

"I think Rivka's doing her speech on what it was like living in Chicago, and it will look like we're copying each other if I talk about that."

"Well, then just talk about moving here from New Jersey, how horribly long the car trip was, and how we finally ended up here."

"I can't tell them about this place."

"Why not?"

"Have *you* told anyone at your school you live here?" I asked her.

"No, way! That's suicidal."

"Exactly! That's why I can't talk about ending up here."

"Yeah, but it's different when you're in middle school. Kids your age don't care about where you live the way high school kids do."

184

"Have you forgotten what it's like to be in middle school?" I asked.

"Okay, why don't you talk about yesterday—how you were supposed to be watching Trinika, and she got lost."

"Great—'I bet you didn't know I lose kids.' I'm sure that will get their attention."

"There you have it!" Phoenix said.

"Thanks for nothing."

"Any time." She started heading back outside, but I stopped her.

"Hey, Phoenix, there's something you need to know about Michael." She looked at me suspiciously, expecting the worst.

"He likes you."

"Yeah, right. He doesn't even know I'm alive."

"Yesterday when he was driving me home, he told me that he likes you, but he's too scared to even talk to you."

"Really? You're not just saying that to get me to do something stupid in front of him?"

"For real. He told me he wants to ask you out."

Phoenix let out a scream. She rushed over to me and gave me a crushing hug. "You're the best sister ever!" she squealed.

I wrestled my way out of her arms and then Phoenix danced her way out the door to go find her soon-to-be new boyfriend. I figured I had maybe 24 hours before things got back to normal and Phoenix went back to thinking I was a not-so-great sister once again.

On Monday, I hoped Rivka and I would go back to normal again too. I figured since she had offered to watch the Jones kids so I could go to Natalie's it meant she wasn't still mad at me. I also figured the scare with Trinika getting lost would set the universe back the way it was, but it seemed Rivka wanted to continue the silent treatment. She wasn't outside when I left for the bus stop in the morning, and when she got on the bus at the motel, she walked right by my seat without even looking at me, even though I had scooted over to make room for her to sit next to me. All morning long, I tried to make eye contact with her in class, but she never bothered to look at me.

Lunch period I was already sitting at the Royal's table when Rivka came out of the food area with Bernice and Monica. Just as they passed our table, Natalie stuck out her foot right in front of Rivka. Rivka tripped over it, lost her balance, and her tray went flying out of her hands. Her lunch went airborne, then came raining down over kids at the surrounding tables. Kids screamed as French fries landed in their hair and on their laps. Along with the screams, there were cheers, hoots, and laughter from the kids who didn't get pelted with food. Natalie, Cassandra and Hailey were all laughing. "Way to go, Motel Girl!" Cassandra yelled out. Rivka's face was as red as the Langstermobile. She ran out of the cafeteria before the lunch monitor had a chance to stop her.

At the end of the lunch period, I hurried out of the cafeteria ahead of the other girls. I ran to Rivka's locker, but she wasn't there. I wanted to find out if she was okay, and let her know I thought what Natalie had done was downright cruel. I checked in the girl's room, but she wasn't there either. When I went to social studies, her desk was empty. She wasn't in any of our classes the rest of the day.

That afternoon on the bus ride home, I thought about what Rivka said about me deserving to be a Royal Ruler because I was just like them. She was wrong. I wasn't like them. Or at least I didn't want to be like them. I didn't want to be mean to other people, or trip them as they walked by and laugh when their tray went flying.

The next day in science class, Natalie turned to me as soon as she sat down at her desk. "Got the homework?"

I shook my head.

"What? You didn't do it?" Natalie stared in disbelief.

"I did my own homework. But I didn't do yours."

"What! Why not?"

"Because, last night I was too busy working on my English speech for tomorrow that I didn't have time to do the science homework for both of us."

"Well give me yours and I'll copy it before the teacher comes in."

"I don't think that's a good idea," I said.

"What? You're just going to let me get a zero for not turning anything in?"

"If I give you my paper and the teacher sees you copying from it, she's going to take it and tear it up, then I'm going to get a zero too."

"Well, if you don't hurry and give it to me, she will, so hurry up!"

Last night while trying to get my own science homework done, I decided it was time to tell Natalie and Cassandra they needed to start doing their own homework. I would offer to tutor them if they needed it, offer to do our homework together, but I wasn't going to do it for them anymore. I knew it wasn't fair to just leave them hanging with no homework today, and I planned to wean them off their dependence on me slowly, but rewriting and practicing my speech had taken longer than I expected. Maybe it was only right I let Natalie copy my homework one last time. I reached in my backpack to get the assignment just as the teacher came in the room and told everyone to pass in their homework.

"Thanks for nothing!" Natalie whispered loudly, then turned her back to me.

It wasn't a good way to start the day, and I knew it was destined to go downhill. Of course, Natalie told Cassandra how I didn't do her homework for her, and Cassandra confronted me during lunch.

"I hope you have my math homework today," she said.

"Listen, Cassandra. You're never going to learn math if I keep doing it for you."

"So, you going to let me take a zero the same way you let Natalie get one this morning?"

"I'll give you last night's answers, but this is the last time. Tonight, I need time to practice my speech for tomorrow, so you're going to have to do your homework yourself."

"Some friend you are."

"I'll tutor you if you need help figuring out how to do the equations, but I can't keep doing them for you every night."

I gave her my math homework to copy, and after that, both she and Natalie ignored me for the rest of the lunch period. A couple of times I tried to contribute to the conversation at the table, but the two of them acted as if they hadn't heard me. Needy Hailey followed their lead and ignored me too. Phoebe, as usual, acted as if she wasn't listening to anyone at the table. I sat through lunch hating my life more than ever. The Royals were all mad at me, Rivka was mad at me. How could I be considered one of the popular kids if I had no friends?

Chapter 26

The next morning, I stopped in the girl's room before homeroom and found Phoebe sitting on the bathroom counter with several blank sheets of notebook paper in front of her. She looked up briefly when I came in, then went back to staring at the blank paper.

"You ready for the big speech today?" I asked.

"Hardly," Phoebe replied, tapping the paper with the end of a pen. "I'm trying to write mine now."

"Really? You haven't written it yet?"

Phoebe got defensive. "It's hard for me to share personal stuff, okay? Besides, everyone thinks they know everything about me anyway, so why bother?"

I hadn't meant to sound accusing; I was just amazed she could write a speech before homeroom and deliver it by third period. As it was, I had rewritten my entire speech last night, and I was nervous as anything that I wouldn't be able to get through it okay with so little practice.

"Have you at least decided on a topic?" I asked.

"No. All anyone wants to hear about is my famous mother."

"Then maybe you should talk about how that makes you feel. Something like, 'I bet you didn't know I hate when you ask me about my mother'."

"Talk about boring."

"Okay...maybe instead of mentioning anything about your mother, what about talking about your father?"

"My father?"

"Yeah. Take away some of the focus everyone has about your mom by talking about your dad. Something like, "I bet you didn't know I have a dad too..." and talk about your relationship with him."

Phoebe shaped her fingers into a pistol and aimed it at me. Thinking she wanted to shoot me, I started backing away. Instead, she snapped her finger pistol and said, "You're okay, California Girl."

By third period I don't think there was a person in our class who wasn't a nervous wreck over giving his or her speech.

"Okay, let's get started," Mrs. Driscoll said with a little smile, which probably was meant to be encouraging, but looked more on the evil side to me. "Who wants to go first?"

If she had asked, "Who wants to be first to stand before the firing squad?" she probably would have met with more enthusiasm from the class. Cassandra was the unlucky one to get called up first. In front of the class she breathlessly announced, "I bet you didn't know I got the leading role in a summer production of *Into the Woods*." Of course, we all knew that already.

Bernice went next and informed us, "I bet you didn't know I own 12 cats," but the cat hair on her clothing every day was a dead giveaway.

Monica gave her speech on having a black belt in karate, which no one knew about and once we found out, she seemed a whole lot more interesting.

Jonathon Parker went up and read from his paper, "I bet you didn't know that I play the piano."

Hailey's speech was, "I bet you didn't know I am 5 feet tall." *Major yawn.*

Aaron Depasko's speech was, "I bet you didn't know I can juggle." *Hmmm...Interesting.* Especially the part when he took out five balls and began juggling them. He was pretty good too—up until the point where Jonathon pretended to sneeze really loud and that threw Aaron off so he missed one of the balls and everyone clapped and cheered when all the other balls clattered to the ground. Aaron ran around picking them all up and said he could do better, but Mrs. Driscoll said he was out of time.

Jake Pellechino's speech was one of the more interesting ones. He started his speech with, "I bet you didn't know I only have four toes on one of my feet."

Everyone laughed, and Jonathon shouted from the back of the room, "Prove it!" whereas Jake took off his shoe and sock and held his foot up in the air to show everyone, while he struggled to balance on the foot with five toes.

"Dude! That is totally gross!" David Gatz said.

All the boys were cracking jokes throughout Jake's speech, while the girls were all grossed out, and a few of them even looked like they wanted to barf as they stared in horror at Jake's bare foot. I'm not kidding when I say the whole room was in chaos over Jake's toes. Everyone wanted to know how he could play soccer so well with only nine toes, and the class kept asking all sorts of other nine-toed questions. Finally, Mrs. Driscoll said we had to move on to the next person.

After Jake's speech, those of us who hadn't gone up yet slunk down in our seats, trying our best not to make eye contact with Mrs. Driscoll.

"Phoebe, let's hear from you next."

Phoebe didn't move from her seat. I wondered if she had been able to finish her speech. She had been frantically writing in first and second periods this morning, and I was certain it had nothing to do with what the teachers were talking about, but the way she was just sitting at her desk now, I started thinking she hadn't been able to come up with something.

"Phoebe?" Mrs. Driscoll called again.

Finally, Phoebe got up and walked slowly to the front of the room. She stared at her paper for a moment before she began to read:

"I bet you didn't know that I was adopted."

A collective gasp went up over the classroom. Ignoring it, Phoebe continued:

"I was adopted by the actress, Blessing Sheffield, who thought she wanted a baby. Unfortunately, she discovered that taking care of a baby and trying to have an acting career at the same time was way more difficult than she expected. She married the first nice guy who

came along, hoping a husband would help take care of the kid. My new father loved me from the start, and was more of a mother to me than my adopted mother was.

When I was two, my mother got the starring role in Bridge Over Juniper and her acting career took off. Marriage and a baby no longer fit in with her lifestyle, and so she left me with my father and grandmother while she went off to L.A. to pursue her acting career.

Many people are either in awe or jealous of me when they find out I'm Blessing Sheffield's daughter, but the truth is, I rarely see her. Once a year over summer vacation I stay at her home in Beverly Hills for two weeks, but during that time, I mostly spend it with the people she employs since she's always busy the whole time I'm there.

The real star in my family is my dad. He could have given me up and sent me back to foster care when Blessing left him, but instead he adopted me and raised me as his own. He's been there for me whenever I've needed him, and he supports me no matter what I do—even when I dye my hair wild colors.

Everyone thinks I'm so popular here at school, but honestly, I don't have any real friends who like me just for me. They like me because of my famous mother. Those of you who are kissing up to me because you want to be friends with someone whose mother is famous are wasting your time. Because another thing I bet you didn't know about me is that my mother, Blessing Sheffield, has never done me any favors. So, don't expect me to do any favors for you because of who my mother is."

The room was eerily quiet when Phoebe finished. If a piece of fuzz fell off someone's clothing right then, I swear, you would have heard it hit the floor. Even Mrs. Driscoll's hands were frozen in mid-clap. No one asked any questions, although everyone was itching to. With her eyes down, Phoebe returned to her seat. Natalie and Cassandra started whispering to each other, and Hailey was on the other side of the room looking like she was going to explode if she didn't get to hear what the two of them were saying to each other.

It was a hard act to follow, and unfortunately, Rivka was the person who had to give her speech right after Phoebe. I guess she didn't slink down low enough in her seat because Mrs. Driscoll called on her.

Rivka took a big gulp and began her speech.

"I bet you didn't know that I used to live in Chicago," she began reading from her paper. *"I lived in Chicago, Illinois for eleven years before my family moved to New York."*

When Rivka was done with her speech, I clapped harder than anyone, but I don't think Rivka noticed. After she sat down, Mrs. Driscoll glanced around to see which condemned students were still left to face execution. Her eyes rested on David Gatz. "David, why don't you go next," she said.

After David finished his speech, Mrs. Driscoll called Anthony DeFranco. Then Miles Clawson. One by one each person slowly made their way up to that dreaded spot in front of the class to deliver the speech they didn't want to do.

In spite of my best effort at looking as if I had already given my speech, Mrs. Driscoll still managed to pick me out. "California, you're next."

With my sweaty hands, I took the paper with my speech and slowly walked to the front of the class. Even though I wasn't looking at anyone, I knew everyone was watching me because everyone watched everyone else as they went up to give their speech. As I felt all eyes on me, I promised myself that I wouldn't stare at the next person giving their speech as they walked up to the front of the class because being watched like that made you start thinking your fly was down or something.

I stood in the front of the room with everyone staring at me, waiting. Taking a deep breath, I began;

"I bet you didn't know that I live in the same motel that Rivka Christianson lives in."

There were no loud gasps from the class or any explosions indicating I had just blown everyone's mind, so I looked up from my paper to see if they heard me correctly. The only thing I noticed was Natalie sitting with her mouth open. I quickly looked back at my paper and plowed on.

"Langster Motel isn't your ordinary motel. It's more like an apartment complex with about a dozen families who have been staying there anywhere from a month to a year. Right now, there are more than twenty-five little kids living in the motel with their families, so there is never a shortage of babysitting jobs for older kids like me and Rivka.

Rivka's father is the manager of the motel and sometimes he lets us have sleepovers in one of the vacant rooms by ourselves. The first time we stayed in a room all night without any adults was a little bit scary, but now we've done it so often, we're used to it. The thing about the vacant room sleepovers is we rarely sleep when we have them. Sometimes we talk all night, sometimes we watch tv, or we'll tell ghost stories, or play Truth or Dare. Sometimes we have sleepovers with our older sisters and it's the four of us sharing the room together, and once in a while when we're not thinking too clearly, we even let a few of the younger kids at the motel join us too.

For Halloween, we had a big party in the recreation room for everyone who lives at the motel. There were games, contests, and so much candy, I was eating it for a month. On Thanksgiving Day, we had a big Thanksgiving dinner with nearly forty people. After we ate, the kids played games, and there was music and even dancing. It was one of the best Thanksgivings I ever had.

You'd think spending Christmas at the motel would be depressing, but it wasn't at all. A few nights before Christmas, a group of about twenty of us went caroling from room to room around the motel, and almost every parent gave us some kind of treat like candy, cookies, or hot chocolate. Christmas Eve we had another big party for everyone at the motel. There was a ten-foot-tall tree in the motel's rec room that all the kids helped to decorate. We had a big meal with everyone helping and so much food made by all the moms at the motel. Since none of the motel rooms have fireplaces, all the kids hung their stockings up in the rec room. It was an awesome sight to see so many stockings in one room.

    The next morning every one of the stockings was filled with candy and presents. After everyone went through their stockings, we all had breakfast together, then we exchanged gifts. Under the tree were tons of presents for every kid there. No one got a new bicycle or anything like that since storing it in a motel room would be too hard, but still... there were some really cool gifts under that tree. After the presents were opened, one of the dads who lives at the motel took out his guitar and we all sang Christmas carols. We spent almost all Christmas day in the motel's rec room. Around 2:00 we had a big dinner of roast beef, ham, turkey, and more food than you can imagine.

    The good thing about living at Langster Motel is you never get lonely because there is always someone around. Everyone who lives at the motel looks out for each other, shares in each other's good fortune when it happens, and we're there to help each other when the going gets tough. Living at Langster is like having a big extended family living close by. Sometimes we get mad at each other--just like any family, but in the end, we make up.

    Would I like to live in a big house with my own room? Of course! Who wouldn't? And someday I know I'll move out of the motel into a house, but meanwhile, living at Langster Motel isn't so bad. It might not be the nicest motel in the area or have the biggest rooms, but it has some of the best people living there—including my best friend, Rivka. Rivka's smart and funny, and she's the most loyal friend a girl could have.

When I'm no longer living at the motel, I hope Rivka and I will still be as close as we are now. I consider her my very best friend in the whole world and anyone who doesn't want to be her friend simply because of where she lives, probably doesn't want to be my friend either."

After what seemed like the longest 10 ½ seconds ever in the history of the planet, Mrs. Driscoll started clapping and the rest of the class joined in. Everyone except Natalie that is. Do you know what she was doing? She was sitting at her desk staring at me with her mouth stuck open like a goldfish with a dislocated jaw. When she saw me looking at her, she quickly closed her mouth and looked up at the ceiling like there was a bug or something that was way more important than anyone's stupid old speech.

"That was wonderful, California," Mrs. Driscoll said. "I had no idea you and Rivka lived in a motel. It sounds like a fun and interesting place to live."

As I walked back to my desk, I snuck a peek at Rivka. She was looking at me and grinning in that smug way she sometimes does as if she predicted all along that I would talk about living in the motel.

At lunch, I knew I wouldn't be sitting at the Royal Rulers' table anymore, considering I not only confessed to living in a motel, but I had also not done Natalie's and Cassandra's homework for them last night. By the time I bought my lunch, all the chairs at the Royals' table were already filled anyway with Natalie, Cassandra, Hailey, and a handful of boys. The girls didn't even bother looking at me when I walked by. I noticed Phoebe wasn't at their table with them. Instead, she was standing in the middle of the cafeteria holding her tray like she couldn't decide where to go.

"Where you sitting, California Girl?" she asked as I came up to her.

"I was thinking about sitting with Rivka today," I said, "...that is, if she'll let me."

"Mind if I join you?"

"No, I don't mind," I said.

"Good. You can tell me more about what it's like living in that motel of yours," she said.

That afternoon, Rivka and I were sitting on the back steps behind the motel. "You were right, Rivka," I said. "Natalie just allowed me to hang out with them so I could do her homework for her. She never liked me."

"I'm not sure Natalie likes anyone except herself," Rivka said.

"You're right again. And I'm sorry I didn't listen to you sooner."

She leaned into me and grinned.

After that, we started going over whose speech was good, and whose speech was majorly lame.

"Your speech was great!" Rivka said. "You even made it sound like the motel wasn't a bad place to live."

"I couldn't make it sound like the dump it really is."

"Nope, you censored it quite well," Rivka said.

"Your speech was good too," I added.

"It would have been better if I had talked about something less boring than about living in Chicago. If I'd known you were going to come clean and talk about the motel, I would have talked about it too."

"You'll probably get a better grade on your Chicago speech than I'll get on mine. You made half the class want to move to Chicago."

"Really? You think so?"

"You really know how to make a topic interesting."

"I seriously doubt I could have made Hailey Ungerman's 'I'm five feet tall' speech interesting," she said.

We both laughed at the memory of the most boring speech *ever*.

"And how about Phoebe being adopted?" Rivka said.

"And that she barely even knows Blessing Sheffield!" I added.

"Looks like the Royal Rulers don't want to hang with her either, now that they know she's no use to their Hollywood brown nosing."

"I don't know, Rivka—I think it's her choice not to hang with them anymore. She didn't seem to like them all that much anyway."

"I told you ages ago, none of them seem to like each other," Rivka said. "I knew something like this was bound to happen sooner or later."

"What? Now you're saying you predicted they were going to have a major breakup?"

"I'm just saying, they never liked each other, that's all."

"Okay, I'll give you that."

"Anyway, I'm glad the whole speech thing is over with," Rivka said.

"Me too."

"When did you decide to give your speech on living at the motel?"

"Last night."

"Really? You waited until last night to decide what to talk about?"

"If you think talking about how tall you are is boring, you should have heard my original talk on being a middle child."

Rivka giggled. "I would have loved it anyway."

"I have to admit, it's a big relief now that we don't have to hide about living here."

Rivka nodded. "Yeah, I hated keeping it a secret."

Just then Pauly and Reza came running over to us.

"Hey, can we get a little privacy here?" Rivka said to her brother.

"This isn't your private motel," said Pauly, plopping down on the step below us. Reza looked up at us nervously before sitting down next to Pauly.

"You know there is no such thing as privacy at Langster Motel," I said to Rivka.

She slapped her forehead. "What was I thinking?"

Pauly's elbow banged against Rivka's foot, and her foot automatically flew out and kicked him. Instead of screaming for his mother like he normally would, Pauly moved a couple of inches away from her.

Just then, Mrs. Jones came around from the front of the motel. She was wearing a hat that had some stuffed bird-like creation draped over the top of it.

"Would y'all mind watching Delilah and Trinika for me?" she asked, coming up to the steps.

I stood up and pulled Rivka to her feet. "Come on. Time to do our thing," I said, climbing over Reza and Pauly on the step below.

"Now promise me y'all keep a good eye on my lil' girls," Mrs. Jones said, standing in front of us.

"Yeah, we will," Rivka said.

"And don't go losing either of *'em*," Mrs. Jones warned.

"We won't," I promised.

Mrs. Jones then went over to the boy's clubhouse and knocked on the door. "Hakeem, *Hunny, yew* in there?"

The door opened and Hakeem popped his head out.

"I'm goin' to the store," his mother told him. "Y'all be *shore* to mind Cali and Rivka, *yew* hear?"

"We're watching Hakeem, too?" Rivka moaned.

"Of course," Mrs. Jones said, surprised that we didn't know keeping an eye on her girls meant keeping an eye on her boy too.

Rivka and I took Trinika's and Delilah's hands and headed to the side yard. Pauly and Reza followed us. The boys ran over to the swings, where Stacey, Georgia and Isabella were all swinging.

"We want a turn," Pauly said to the girls.

"Tough, we were here first," Stacey said.

Trinika and Delilah ran over to the sandbox and we sat down under a tree. Mrs. Rivera came out of her room with Gabby and Hector. The kids ran over to the swings, and Mrs. Rivera came clickity-clack over to us. "Girls, keep an eye on Hector and Gabby for me, will you?" she asked.

"We can't. We're already watching the Jones kids," I said.

"I'll be back in about an hour," Mrs. Rivera said, as if she hadn't heard me. She started to walk away and then as an afterthought added, "Oh...and Roberto is around here somewhere. You better go find him to make sure he doesn't get into trouble."

We watched as she and Mrs. Jones got in the Riveras' car together. Even before the vehicle was out of the parking lot, Hector and Pauly began tormenting the girls by tugging on the swings to get them to stop. Suddenly, the whole playground was filled with screaming as the girls yelled at them to stop, and the boys yelled back to say they wanted a turn swinging.

Rivka threw up her hands. "Why is it we always have to watch these kids all the time? Why can't Shannon and Phoenix do it? Or even Stacey and Georgia?"

"Haven't you figured it out yet, Rivka?" I asked.

"Figured out what?"

"We're popular."

"Ha!" Rivka snorted.

"Think about it, Rivka. The parents all like us because we always watch their kids. If we're not around to watch their kids, they can't go anywhere or they have to drag their kids with them. The parents don't want to take their kids with them, and the kids don't want to be dragged on errands. They'd rather stay here with us, playing outside. Without us to watch them, all the kids and their parents would be miserable. So, when it comes down to it, you and I are the most popular residents of Langster Motel."

"You mean we've been trying to become popular at school and it turns out we've been popular all along right here at Langster Motel?"

"Pretty much," I replied. "But with your sixth sense you knew that all along, right?"

"Nope, never saw that one coming," Rivka admitted.

"Well, Miss Co-Popularity," I said standing up. "We better go break up the fight over by the swings before our fans pulverize each other."

We headed across the yard with Rivka screaming, "HECTOR! PAULY! LEAVE THOSE GIRLS ALONE OR WE'RE GONNA FEED YOU TO THE COYOTES!"

About the Author

Cindy Sabulis first began writing her debut novel *Living at Langster Motel* when she was just eleven years old. Well...sort of. The story was actually a byproduct of a sixth-grade class assignment. Cindy had to write her autobiography, the "tell-all" story about her eleven-year history. At the time, Cindy was temporarily living in a motel with her family, so motel life played a prominent part in her finished assignment. When she moved out of the motel and changed schools, her autobiography was left behind at her old school, so Cindy decided not only to rewrite it, but to expand on it with more stories about the motel where she lived. As a young adult, Cindy took those pre-teen, autobiographical writings about motel life, and used them to create fictional stories about kids who lived in motels. *Living at Langster Motel* is a blending of several different unpublished stories she previously wrote decades before.

In addition to this book, Cindy is the author of five nonfiction books. Prior to writing books, Cindy worked for many years as a freelance writer and a contributing editor for magazines and newspapers.

If you enjoyed reading *Living at Langster Motel,* be sure to recommend it to your friends and please share a review for it on Amazon, Goodreads, and other online sites.

The author can be found on the web at:
www.cindysabulis.com
www.facebook.com/LivingatLangsterMotel

Made in the USA
Middletown, DE
21 April 2022

64494730R00119